The Roman of the North

Celtic Highland Maidens

Michelle Deerwester-Dalrymple

The Roman of the North

Copyright 2021 Michelle Deerwester-Dalrymple All rights reserved
ISBN: 9798408781744
Imprint: Independently published

Proofreading by Phoenix Book Promo

All rights reserved. In accordance with the U.S. Copyright Act of 1976, the scanning, uploading, distribution, or electronic sharing of any part of this book without the permission of the author constitutes unlawful piracy of the author's intellectual property. If you would like to use the material from this book, other than for review purposes, prior authorization from the author must be obtained. Copies of this text can be made for personal use only. No mass distribution of copies of this text is permitted.

This book is a work of fiction. Names, dates, places, and events are products of the author's imagination or used factiously. Any similarity or resemblance to any person living or dead, place, or event is purely coincidental.

Chapter One: The North	7
Chapter Two: First Impressions	19
Chapter Three: Plotting	25
Chapter Four: Latrines	29
Chapter Five: Gossip and Rumors	45
Chapter Six: Information	57
Chapter Seven: Drunkards	63
Chapter Eight: Urgent Encounters	67
Chapter Nine: Secrets	81
Chapter Ten: Taking the Time	87
Chapter Eleven: Confrontations	99
Chapter Twelve: Commitments	113
Chapter Thirteen: A Plan in Place	125
Chapter Fourteen: A New Home	137
An Excerpt from The Maiden of the Stones	143
An Excerpt from To Dance in the Glen	145
A Note on History	151
A Thank You to My Readers –	153
About the Author	155
Also by the Author:	157

The Roman of the North

The Roman of the North

What is the measure of a man's honor?

The Roman of the North

Chapter One: The North

Summer 210 AD — Northern Caledonii Tribal lands – Scottish Highlands – Antoine's Wall

The clanging sound of swords and armor echoed between the green hills that cast long shadows on the narrow glen and darkened the lush trees.

Antonius shivered under his tunic as a breeze kicked up, rustling the leaves and chilling him to the bone. His cock and ballocks, protesting at the chill, shriveled painfully into his groin to hide from the breeze. Even in high summer, this brutal remote land in the barbarian north never warmed. Antonius missed the hot, arid summers of Rome, and the dark-haired Mera who had promised to wait for him. She spoke the words with her mouth, but the lie rested in her eyes. She was too beautiful to wait for a poor legionnaire, especially with the butcher's son, Marcus, chasing her heels at the forum market.

Memories of his time back in the outskirts of Rome warmed him little. As the third son of a poor market vendor selling cheap trinkets, what options did he have? None, but to join the Roman Legion in their call to send an Eagle standard to combat the northern barbarians. Now, instead of sleeping on a pallet, sweating in the Roman summer heat and dreaming of Mera, he was freezing on a military pallet, dreaming of his next meal.

Antonius's legs pimpled under the cool breeze, and he again wished that he might wear his *bracae* pants under his tunic. The guard commander permitted it in the winter, when snow encased this land like a bad senator's wig, but when leaves and grass sprouted under a pale summer sun? Never. Tunic and sandals only.

So instead, Antonius shivered as he walked, marching through yet another set of foothill near his fort, searching for the gods knew what. His commander had instructed them to keep their eyes open.

Open for what? That he didn't tell them.

All he knew was his *contubernuim* troupe of eight presently marched north of the wall, a place off limits, according to the loose terms of the Caledonii peace treaty.

Antonius didn't care. He hated this place. He hated these barbaric Caledonii. He hated this assignment in the far north, away from the warmth of home.

In his estimation, they should just burn it all down and let the gods figure it out.

A plop of chilled rain splashed on his nose, just under the nose guard of his helmet.

He clenched his jaw.

This cold forsaken place, it probably won't even burn, anyway.

He wasn't the only one grumbling, thankfully. Perhaps if the commander heard enough of them griping about this march, he'd turn them around, south to the wall. If they were lucky, they might make it back in time for the evening meal.

The only redeeming part of that prospect was the chance that dinner would still be warm, even if it was only thin gruel and bread.

At least it'd be warm gruel.

Lost in his thoughts, his mind didn't quite register the movement on the far side of the glen until the movement brightened and a swath of color shifted in the trees. Antonius slowed his march and focused his eyes. The glen was narrow and ended in a thick tree line at the base of a stony hill. Bright red and a rich blue moved in the trees.

Then the man and two young women emerged, and his entire Centauriae stopped, the sudden halt of their clanging armor almost louder than the sound of their shuffling feet and questioning chatter.

They were close enough to the trio for Antonius to register the shock on their faces.

And he knew why the shock was there. The Roman army was somewhere they weren't supposed to be.

Maybe a lone set of Caledonii was what Antonius was supposed to keep an eye open for.

The two groups stared at each other for the space of several heartbeats, before a few Roman soldiers broke ranks and rushed the trio. The Caledonii man threw the spear he held before turning to run into the trees with the two women. The spear bounced off a soldier's shield and was flung to the side like an irritating bug.

"Halt!" a stern, powerful voice carried in the air, and the few soldiers who had broken ranks immediately stopped, keeping their eyes on the tree line.

"Fall in!" the voice commanded, and those errant soldiers returned to their places.

The Prefect had instructed the lower ranks to keep their distance from any locals, as established by the treaty.

Not that the Romans had abided by that treaty at all.

If they had, they wouldn't be on the north side of Antoine's wall now would they? Not even scouts were supposed to step north of the wall, per the treaty. Sentries and a few random sentry towers that were ill-crafted and too widely spaced to be any good — that was all with regards to the guards on the wall. The legion at Antoine's wall was mired in shit.

The men fell in. Antonius, however, didn't focus on the rank and file in front of him. Something about these people they'd found, their shockingly bright hair, their muscular, barely covered bodies marked with red and blue tattoos in odd swirls. Only, their coloring wasn't what caught his attention the most.

No, it was the fierce gaze of the shorter woman, the one with the wild shock of hair the color of an Alban sunset.

She didn't turn as quickly as her two companions. Rather, she kept her gaze riveted on the armor-clad men, as though she was challenging them to face her, her face a wash of pure hatred.

Antonius chewed at his lip, hiding a smile.

Gumption, his mother had called that look, that trait. Gumption, the will to stand up in the face of something dire, to challenge authority.

Antonius never had the gumption, not the type his mother spoke of so highly. Though he'd always wanted it, or at least the opportunity to see if he had it. He was almost jealous of the woman's gumption.

The marching resumed its steady cadence, turning back in a south-easterly direction toward the Roman camp south of the wall.

"Antonius, Cassius, Titus, Androdinus! Front and center!"

The four soldiers neared the wall, their fort a welcome sight as the misty rain increased. They hadn't had to walk very far, and for that Antonius was grateful. His stomach rumbled.

Yet, now his guard commander called him forward. Their Centurion, the commander of the entire cohort of the three forts at this part of Antoine's Wall awaited them, his feathery helm shining in the rain.

"Your commander tells me you came upon Caledonii locals this afternoon. Our presence on the north side of the wall will not be tolerated. You must find these locals and bring them to me. They cannot tell their leaders what they have seen."

A simple enough task, but one that sent Antonius's stomach to his feet. Titus, one of the more ardent Roman soldiers in his Centauriae, however, smiled widely, knowingly.

Bring them to the Centurion? That meant only one thing. They would be sent off to become slaves to the Roman Empire. Antonius might despise this northern land and its people, but the viscous bite of slavery never sat well with him. He'd seen too much violence wrought upon men and women, young and old, whose only crime was to be captured by a more powerful enemy.

He wouldn't wish slavery on his worst enemy, even if that worst enemy were these Caledonii. Once again, it didn't smack of honor to him.

The Roman army here at the wall was not abiding by the terms of the treaty by any measure, and Antonius feared what his Centurion, or the higher-up Prefect might do to twist this event against the Caledonii. Or what would happen when these northern barbarians figured the treachery out. These were not the weaker Celts or Gaels of the continent.

These northern island tribal people were unlike anything he'd encountered in his life.

He feared that the mighty Roman army, strung thin at this far recess of the world, would regret their decision to break the treaty. Antonius might not have the gumption of which his mother spoke, but he did have honor. And invading these people and breaking the treaty was not honorable. And his Centurion was forgetting something important, something Antonius kept at the forefront of his mind at all times.

These giant northerners were not ones to be trifled with.

The trees were thick on the east side of the glen where he had been assigned to hunt. He blinked against the mist as he moved farther into the trees. His prey was those three Caledonii, and he prayed to his gods that he wasn't the unfortunate soul to find them, to bring them back to face a horrific future in Rome, to break that treaty and risk his life against the barbarians.

What retribution might these northerners take against the man who absconded with their people? There was a reason the Roman army had constructed Antoine's wall. This man and these women were sons and daughters of Caledonii villages, perhaps of leaders and chieftains.

Antonius would be fortunate to keep his head off a pike if discovered. The Roman army believed themselves to be the most powerful on earth, but if that was so, then why did they form a treaty with the northerners? Here, spread out so far and with few reinforcements, the Roman army was not the most powerful entity, though most soldiers in his Centauriae were loath to admit it.

No, here in the north, these barbarians reigned. And they had put the Roman army in its place.

A rustling in the brush pulled Antonius from his dismal thoughts. *A pheasant? A badger?* he hoped.

He scanned the trees, and a wisp of purple-blue, barely discernible in the dying light, caught his eye.

Oh no.

Definitely not an animal.

He stepped through the trees to find an interesting sight that froze him where he stood in the spongy undergrowth.

The man who'd thrown his spear at them was draped between the two women who half-carried, half-dragged the man through the woods. Antonius dropped his gaze to the man's legs, noting one foot twisted awkwardly. No running on that ankle. He was impressed by the women for their undertaking. Having done this very thing before, Antonius knew how difficult it could be to tow a man through the woods. Too many obstacles, too many curves and stones and divots in the land.

They also froze when he appeared, and for a moment, much like in the glen, they stared at each other from an arm's length away. Then the taller woman with wavy, reddish-blonde hair moved smoothly and withdrew a short sword from her belt before he could move and take up guard. Antonius stiffened at the sight. He'd heard rumors of the Caledonii warrior women — many of the barbarians the Romans had battled in these northern climes fought alongside their women — but he hadn't expected the woman to be so prepared for battle. Why hadn't he drawn his own *gladius* sword in response?

"What do ye want? Do ye no' know of the treaty?" She pointed the tip of the sword at his leather-clad chest.

Antonius spoke a broken version of the northern language — it was required as part of his training, but her thick brogue made her difficult to understand. He didn't speak the language well, after all.

"I'm searching for you," he answered as best he could, hoping she understood him. The other, shorter woman with brilliant crimson curls spoke to her friend so quickly, Antonius missed it.

The sword-wielding woman's eyes cut from him to her friend and back to him. She thrust the sword at his chest again.

"How many are there of you?" she asked, thankfully speaking her language slowly.

Antonius took barely a minute to consider his answer. He didn't want to be the one to cause rife with the Caledonii, who gravely outnumbered the Romans and could easily overpower them, even with all the military strength of the Roman war machine behind them. He also didn't want to die right here in this wet forest.

"Four soldiers are looking for you."

The tip of the blade shifted from the protection of his leather-studded metal chest plate. Metal armor often froze or stuck in the far northern climes, but even when not in combat, their leaders demanded they wear armor, lest the legionaries grow weak or forget how to fight in it. Though solid enough, the armor exposed his neck, which was protected only by a red scarf tied in a front knot where her blade point now rested.

He flicked his eyes to the smaller woman, the one who seemed less aggressive. His life, it seemed, might hang on her words regarding him.

"And what happens when you find us?"

Antonius chewed at his lip, his mind reeling. She'd surely slay him where he stood if she knew the truth. But if he could help them, perhaps he'd escape with his life intact. Maybe the truth was what he needed to share with them.

"I'm supposed to subdue you, bring you back to the fort, where you will be shipped off to Rome to make an example of you."

Blatant honesty seemed the wisest approach. The shorter woman paled at his words and flicked a worried gaze to her sword-wielding friend.

"You think you can take a Caledonii?" Her tone was sharp, confident of her skills, but from the look of the shorter woman, she didn't agree with her friend. The wild-haired woman spoke again. The sword-woman answered back, just as fast, and Antonius lost their conversation. The woman turned her attention back to Antonius, awaiting his answer.

"Not by myself, no. You have me at a, um, disadvantage." He glanced down at the sword pointed at his neck for emphasis before continuing. "Yet, I can help you escape, if you promise to let me leave with my life."

The woman lifted the sword so the cool metal touched under his chin. "And why would we trust you, a Roman?"

"Because you are correct. We have broken the treaty by being on this side of the wall, and I would try to rectify that."

The woman spat on the ground next to his *caligae* boot. "Why should I believe you? Your words ring false."

At this, Antonius shifted his eyes to gaze at the shorter woman. Her pale face only accentuated the spray of cinnamon freckles across her nose and her green-gold eyes that studied him with intensity.

If he didn't have a sword at his throat, he'd believed that she could find him intriguing, studying him like some of the ancient Greeks had studied the stars.

And for a moment, he lost himself her in gaze. It had been a long while since he'd had a woman, and the way she looked at him . . .

The sword woman spoke again, and he turned his head.

"Why will I help you?" he asked, hoping he'd heard her correctly. She nodded. "Because I know what your people can do, how you can fight, and the treaty is weak at best. I'd not be responsible for the retribution your people would have on the Romans if we broke the treaty."

The leaves rustled above him, and he spun his head, fearing his fellow Centauriae had discovered him. No, only the breeze in the last rays of the sun. Soon it would be full dark, and he was still on the wrong side of the wall.

"Can you leave the other way, so we might return to our village?" the shorter woman finally spoke slowly enough that he could understand her. The sword woman whipped her head around and glared at her.

"Muireall! Dinna speak to him!"

The shorter woman rolled her eyes at her friend. The man dangling from her arm groaned a bit, but kept himself otherwise quiet as the two women spoke.

"Gwyneth! Ye canna risk killing a Roman and keeping the treaty intact. No more than he can kill us and do the same. And what would your father think, if ye threatened that treaty?"

The sword woman, Gwyneth, seemed to find veracity in Muireall's words. Her puffed chest deflated, and she dropped the sword to her side. Whoever this woman's father was, he had to be powerful. A leader, or a chieftain even?

"My friend speaks the truth. I canna risk that treaty. If ye can promise we go our separate ways, then we'll keep this silent. Can ye agree to the same?"

Muireall's green-gold eyes pleaded with him. She didn't need to — Gwyneth's plan was a sound one to him.

"Yes, I can do that," he answered quickly, eager to keep his head upon his shoulders. "I find your plan most agreeable."

Gwyneth pursed her lips at him and waved her sword to her left. "Then go back the way ye came and tell your companions that no Caledonii were found this way."

Antonius bowed slightly, and with a faint glance at Muireall to burn her image into his mind, he spun around and strode swiftly through the woods until he reached the glen. He didn't look back, but waited for the spear to thrust into his back. When it didn't, he released a deep breath and rushed past the tree line. There he found the hard-faced Titus as his fellow soldier emerged from the brush to the north.

"Hail, Antonius! Did you find any barbarians in your searches?"

Antonius shook his head. "No, Titus. And I see you fared no better than I. Perchance they turned back and headed west. Cassius may have had better luck."

Titus narrowed his eyes at him. "Odd. They seemed to have gone in your same direction. How could you have missed them?"

"I didn't see them." Though he tried to sound convincing, Antonius could hear the hesitation in his voice. And if he heard it, then so did Titus. The tall legionnaire's face tightened to match his eyes, before tipping his head over his shoulder.

"Let us head back to the fort. The Centurion wanted us back by dark."

"Yes. We are useless soldiers if a band of Caledonii sneaks up on us in the dark whilst we are on the wrong side of the wall."

Titus clapped his hand hard against Antonius's shoulder, a little too hard. "You fear being on the wrong side of the wall. If Roman soldiers couldn't take on the Caledoniis, do you think our commanders would risk us being here?"

Antonius again had to force himself not to glance over his shoulder. He didn't answer Titus's question. If Gwyneth and her friend Muireall were any indication, the four Roman soldiers would be in trouble if caught on the north side of the wall indeed.

They made it back in time to eat the remnants of lukewarm, wild game gruel and dry bread before Antonius found his bed.

But this night, instead of shivering under his thin blanket, his skin burned warm at the memory of the short, curvy, wild-haired woman. Try as he might, he couldn't remove the image of the barbarian woman from his mind. She provided a new fantasy as his hand found his cock, and then again in his dreams as he slept.

Chapter Two: First Impressions

"Ye spoke to him far too much, Muireall," Gwyneth chided her friend gently from the other side of Evan's sagging form. Trying to run on his twisted ankle had worn him out and only made his agony worse. Now he was suffering for it. They hoped Ayla might work some healing magic and treat it so he'd suffer no long-term damage.

"Dinna scold her, Gwyneth," Evan grumbled back at her. "She was just making her voice heard. Some of us think before drawing a sword, aye?"

Muireall might not have been able to see it, but she was certain Gwyneth was rolling her eyes at Evan's comment. Gwyneth was not a woman who enjoyed being told what to do at all. Partly due to her inner traits blessed by the goddess, partly as an entitlement as a daughter of the chieftain.

"I merely think we canna trust a Roman as far as I can throw him. The less we speak to him, the better."

"I thought he was kind enough," Muireall interjected, tired of being the silent third wheel of the conversation. And he had been kind, if he didn't betray them to his leaders as soon as he left the grove of trees. She didn't know why, but Muireall had the idea that he was a man of honor who'd keep his vow, enemy or no.

Gwyneth snorted. "Ye find all manner of injured animals kind enough. Just dinna be dragging this one home. We've had enough interactions with the Romans to last awhile."

Muireall snapped her mouth shut. Her friends spoke a heavy truth. Gwyneth wasn't only referring to this evening, but also about her sister's marriage the previous year to a Roman, of all people. Gwyneth's father, the chieftain, still visibly chaffed every time he thought on it. It seemed maybe Gwyneth did, too.

Kilsyth village was not much farther through the woods. They dropped Evan off at his parent's wheelhouse with a promise from Gwyneth to send her sister Ayla over to look at the ankle. As their village healer, she was a miracle worker at times. Evan's mother's face softened with relief at Gwyneth's promise.

"What will ye tell your father?" Muireall pried as they walked toward their own wheelhouses in the village. They reached Gwyneth's first and paused before getting too close.

"I will tell him most of the truth, that we were chasing game and Evan tripped on a loose stone, twisting his ankle. I fear I must tell him that we did see some Romans in the distance, though. I'll keep my promise not to mention we actually spoke to one, but better that my father be prepared if the Romans are trespassing where they shouldn't."

Muireall nodded. "I will tell my family the same, only leaving out anything about the Romans." She turned to leave when Gwyneth grasped her *léine*.

"I saw the way that Roman looked at ye," she said, a note of caution in her voice. "I would advise ye to forget ye ever saw him at all. He's no lame animal to bring home and care for. Trust me on this. No father wants to see his daughter with a foul Roman."

Nay, they didn't. Gwyneth spoke from experience in her own home.

Still, something about how that Roman's eyes gazed at her, dark like a loch in the night. She patted her friend's hand.

"He's likely no' seen a woman in months. Most likely he's taking in a look to savor whilst he abuses himself this night, I expect."

Gwyneth held her gaze for a moment longer, then cracked a tight smile and nodded. "Likely so. Filthy Romans. I pity that ye might find yourself the subject of his lurid fantasies." She kissed Muireall's forehead and then lifted her skirts, racing for her doorway.

Muireall watched her leave, then tipped her head up at the sky before walking toward home. The night was as dark as the Roman's eyes, and just as deep and sparkling.

She might never see him again, the goddess willing, but she had enjoyed being the focus of his attention, limited though it might have been.

And if he used her for his fantasies this eve, well, she didn't mind that much, either.

She might do the same with his image.

Though he expected the call, Antonius was surprised it didn't come for nearly two days after their excursion beyond the wall.

"And you saw nothing, not one at all? Even though your guard commander indicated that was the direction the Caledonii departed in?" Doubt filled the Prefect's voice. This was a man who served under the Legate and was in charge of three Centauriae at Antoine's Wall. He was not a man to be trifled with, and here Antonius was, trifling with him.

Antonius stood at attention, his hands clasped behind his back, his eyes straight ahead. He was grateful for the attention stance — it prevented him from fidgeting while the lies fell readily from his lips.

"No, Prefect Didius. I searched the trees all the way to the base of the foothill. Nothing."

The Prefect tapped his finger on the parchment in front of him. "I find that hard to believe. According to our maps, a Caledonii village, a large and important one, lies just beyond the wood to the east. And yet you saw no sign of them?"

Antonius kept his eyes fixed on the draping tent wall behind the Prefect. "No, nothing. They must have run, and they know these lands better than we do. I'm sure they know the quickest way back to their village, if indeed they went that way."

Prefect Didius tapped the map again but didn't ask another question. He nodded his head at the guard commander. "Send in the next legionnaire." His eyes came back to Antonius. "You're dismissed."

Antonius exited and walked several steps before he started breathing normally. A thin film of sweat covered his forehead, and he wiped it away. Had the Prefect seen it? Had it given him away?

No one followed him back to his own tent, so he was probably safe.

He had tried to forget the Caledonii he'd met in the woods, that red-headed woman who commanded his gaze. She'd haunted his dreams.

Why? What was it about her?

Probably because she was the only woman he'd seen in months. Barbarian or no. That's what he tried to tell himself.

But then, why hadn't her friend, the sword woman, done the same?

Muireall. Her name rolled around in his brain. The way the sword woman had spoken it, rough and growling, almost like a dog, so different from the clear and clipped names of Rome.

He passed Titus on his way back to his tent. His fellow soldier bore a serious face as he marched across the grass.

"Meeting with the Prefect?" Antonius asked. Titus started, as if he hadn't seen Antonius.

"Yes, something serious. I think he's upset we didn't find the locals."

Antonius raised an eyebrow. "I just spoke with him. He might be upset but didn't appear overly angered."

Titus's jaw twitched, and Antonius had the sudden awareness that something more was going on. Something that the Prefect didn't share with him. Didius might have listened to his story, but that didn't mean the commander believed him. And neither did Titus.

"Yes, well, the guard commander who called for me made it sound differently. What with you not having seen the barbarians." Titus shifted his eyes around the tents. He was avoiding Antonius's gaze.

Antonius swallowed at the sudden lump in his throat, a sudden realization paining him. The Prefect wasn't going to let those locals go. He would hunt them down if necessary. Antonius was certain. The Prefect was not a man to be trifled with. But why would he do all that, when it would certainly break the already tenuous treaty?

He didn't know what the Prefect's plan was in wanting to find Muireall or Gwyneth and their friend, but if he learned of the direction they'd went, he'd have Romans lie in wait until they saw the barbarians again. A foolish desire to win, to show the locals that the Romans were powerful enough to bend them to Rome's will, to mobilize the full power of the Roman army in the north and bring the barbarians to heel. Antonius had seen the Prefect do it before.

And if that happened, Didius would also think that Antonius lied to him about finding the Caledonii to the east. That would not end well for Antonius.

The Prefect would send Muireall away from her family to be a slave in the strange, hot city of Rome. Antonius couldn't begin to imagine it. He was having a hard enough time adjusting to this foreign place, and he'd volunteered to come here.

To be taken against his will? He shuddered under his leather chest plate.

Surely that was a fate worse than any death he might imagine.

Antonius watched Titus until he ducked inside the Prefect's lush tent, then he turned toward his own tent.

The Prefect and his foolish quests weren't his concern. What could he do against the might of the Roman Army?

Chapter Three: Plotting

But his mind wouldn't let it go, and that night, as Antonius tried to sleep, his mind tortured him with images of the pale Muireall and her burning eyes. Something about the woman tugged at him, marked his brain and wouldn't let go.

He couldn't understand it. He'd had women before, Mera included. His fascination with the Caledonii woman was more than just middling interest or a fantasy for self-pleasure. The way she looked at him, as if she was as curious about him as he was about her . . .

Titus had returned to their tent shortly after the evening meal and went right to his cot, removed his armor, and laid down facing the wall.

Whatever the Prefect had told him wasn't sitting well, and he didn't want Antonius to know.

That could only mean one thing. The Prefect wasn't done with the Caledonii they'd encountered in the glen.

Antonius rolled onto his back and crossed his arms under his head.

What if he could warn the wild woman? Find her and warn her that his Prefect had turned his attention to them, to make an example or meet some twisted idea of Roman Imperialism with these three. Would that save Muireall and her friends from a dire fate?

But how? How could he do that?

Antonius turned his gaze without moving his head, studying the men snoring in the tent. Daybreak was several hours away. Could he find which way they went? Track them? Warn her and make it back before morning wake-up?

Maybe. If her village wasn't too far. He knew what direction they left in, and he could at least start looking for her, wait until she was by herself. As long as no Caledonii warriors, or that sword woman, discovered him . . .

It was risky, but so was being a soldier. And if he tried, if even he failed, then he could live with himself. Antonius didn't think he'd be able to live with himself unless he at least tried. Better to fail as a man of repute than to do nothing can permit iniquity to thrive. And his leaders of his Centauriae were not being honorable.

Another round of snoring convinced him. Leaving his armor plates and shield behind so he might move more swiftly and quietly in the dark, he tucked his knife into his belt and crouched low to the ground, creeping past the other soldiers snoring on their pallets, and made it silently to the tent flap.

Avoiding sleeping men was one thing. Avoiding the nighttime sentries was quite another. He peered down the crushed grass walkway, searching for any guards. The walkways to his right and left were dark and empty. The entire camp slept.

In a low crouch, Antonius snaked past the tents toward the wall. He was fortunate in that, as a lowly legionnaire, his tent was near the rear of the camp, farther down from the wall and away from the Prefect and Centurion's tents. If he could find cover at the wall, he might hide from the fort sentries as he scaled over.

He stood in the shadows of the last tent, studying the stone barrier. A dense willow draped its sagging boughs over the top of the low-lying wall, barely visible in this half-moon night.

Perfect.

Looking out for any sentries or guards who might surprise him, Antonius waited until the pathway was clear, then ran for all he was worth. He reached the hip-high wall, ducked under the draping willow bough, and leapt over in one smooth movement. He landed easily on his boot-clad toes.

Landed on Caledonii land.

Alone.

He took a deep breath and started northeast in the direction he believed Muireall and her friends departed. He had little knowledge of the area, and even less awareness of his surroundings in the dark. Leaving the safety of the willow, he let the stars and the nearly full moon be his guide.

Tracking a days-old trail at night was not the same as daytime tracking, and it took a while before Antonius found any hint of their trail from the days before. Even then, he wasn't certain and had to hope that he was on the right track.

Once he found what he believed to be the correct trail, he tried to fix it so it no longer looked like the trail headed north-east by throwing a hand full of wet leaves over the shallow imprints he found in the muddy pathway. He squinted at the pathway in front of him that led into the trees. Noting the steps with a drag line in the middle — the man's twisted foot mayhap?— Antonius followed it as far as he dared that night.

But he lost it when the grass on the path thickened in the woods. When he still hadn't found anything after an hour, he doubled back the way he'd came and made his way back to camp.

He wasn't born yesterday, though. He'd left a sign for himself where he'd lost the trail, tying a narrow strip of red linen from his tunic on a low brush.

He'd pick up the trail at the spot he marked tomorrow night and try again.

Chapter Four: Latrines

Antonius made it back to the camp only an hour before sunup. This time, he managed to fall asleep right away, only to be shocked back into awareness at the sound of the morning horn. He rubbed his face, trying to wake up, when Titus smacked him on the head.

"Get up. We've got work to do today."

"What work?" Antonius started to ask as he shoved himself up from the drowning pull of sleep, but Titus was already out of the tent.

The open flap let a surprisingly brilliant and rare ray of light pierce the tent, and Antonius blinked and raised a hand to cover his eyes. Was he wrong, or did Titus seem angry this morn?

Rolling out of bed, Antonius groaned to himself. If anyone should be angry, it was Antonius and his lack of sleep. It was going to be a long day.

He found Titus at the front of the line, waiting for him. Not in full armor, but a worn tunic and red scarf knotted around his thick neck. He tipped his head to Antonius.

"Leave the armor. We have latrine duty today." The tone of his voice let Antonius know how irate Titus was at this lowly duty. He blamed their unfortunate task on Antonius.

Antonius cringed as well, but didn't blame him a bit. Only the worst of soldiers, or newest recruits, were assigned latrine duty! What was the Prefect thinking? Had Antonius's subterfuge been discovered? If so, why was the golden boy, Titus, assigned the duty as well?

Antonius returned his leather chest plate to his tent and wrapped his own scarf around his lower face. Then he walked back to Titus and hoped the man would be much more conversant than he was thus far.

The sun beat down on their heads as they dug at the southern end of the latrine, allowing run-off to flow, for lack of a better word, and move the foetid refuse out of the primary usage area. And the latrine was unfortunately well used. The thin linen did little to staunch the unbelievable stench emanating from the putrid work. While Antonius was grateful it wasn't raining, a bit less of a warm sun might have helped keep the rancid odor under control.

Titus worked with silent anger, an ire that Antonius could sense as much as he could smell the latrine. Finally, nearing noon, Titus stabbed his shovel in the loose topsoil.

"What in Jupiter's testicles did you do, Antonius, that you couldn't find them? Do you think anyone really believed that shit story?" he finally asked.

Antonius slowed his digging but didn't stop. His mind raced, first from the fiery-eyed woman, then to his fellow soldier and the lie he'd have to tell.

"Me? What about you? None of us found them! And it's not like these people don't know their own land. I'm sure they hid their tracks or took a way back to their village that we don't know about." Then Antonius speared his own shovel into the dirt. "And what of it? We were in the wrong, Titus. Don't forget that. We shouldn't have tracked them, anyway."

"That's not the point. The Prefect wants to know where all the Caledonii and their villages are, and you losing them, one injured no less, didn't help him. How can we defeat these barbarians, bring them under the banner of Rome, if you let them wander away? Our goal is the glory of Rome, after all."

The heat and disgusting work of the day was forgotten as Antonius's mind churned over at Titus's words. The glory of Rome? What glory was there in subduing and subjugating people who'd lived on their own land for generations? What honor was there in decimating entire peoples, first on the mainland, and now here on this remote isle? To what end? Antonius squared off against the slightly taller, more slender man.

"What do you mean, bring them under the banner of Rome? We had to build a second wall to keep them away from us. We have a treaty in place. There's no honor in breaking it. Surely, the Prefect must be mad to think—"

Titus chest bumped him as he looked down his nose. "Your ideas of honor? It is an honor to serve Rome. And both sides have not fully adhered to the treaty, as you well know. Prefect Didius is doing what the Legatus has commanded, what Emperor Severus wants, straight from Rome. The walls are temporary. Even a dullard like yourself should have realized that." Titus chest bumped him again.

Antonius let the insult go — he'd heard it before. Because he wasn't much of a talker in the camp, he was perceived as slow. But he'd learned that puffed up men often spoke more than was good for them. Antonius had realized long ago to hold his tongue unless he had something of import to say.

That chest bump, though . . .What was Titus trying?

Antonius stepped forward in more of a push than a chest bump. Two could play Titus's game.

"You could be executed if you're found to be helping the painted barbarians, you fool. And now look what you got me into, shoveling shit on a hot day!" There, Titus finally voiced his suspicions out loud. He did believe Antonius to be aiding the barbarians. He just couldn't prove it, which was why Antonius still had his head upon his shoulders.

At this, Titus shoved at Antonius's chest. Antonius lost his footing but had the sense to grab Titus's arm before he slipped into the newly dug latrine.

The only upside was they had just started digging that day, so the new trench for the latrine was only starting to fill with waste.

The bad news was they both fell into it — Antonius on his back and Titus landing with his face in the putrid mud.

"You donkey's ass!" Titus screeched as he tried to wipe his face clean.

The smell consumed all of Antonius's senses, burning his eyes, nose and throat, warm and squishy between his fingers. He swallowed back the bile that shot into his throat. Then he shifted to shove Titus off him, but the tainted mud was slippery, and they both floundered in the muck. Titus lifted a fist to punch Antonius, who managed to roll away before the fist landed, flinging muck all over the both of them. Titus struck only soft, foetid mud and roared his irritation. Antonius tried to regain his footing, but only reached his knees in the disgustingly warm muck before Titus launched at him.

Poor Titus didn't realize how slippery the muck was, and slipped, this time falling full face first into the feces-mud mix. Antonius leaned back on his heels, grimacing at Titus's misfortune and gagging at the mere thought of Titus's mouth full of feces. How did Titus not puke? Antonius crab-walked backwards. He sure as Hades didn't want to fight in this shitpit.

"Stop, Titus," he said, breathing shallowly through his mouth. "I don't know what's possessed you this day, but I have no desire to roll around in shit. Leave off. I'm done digging. I have no care if I'm flogged. I'm off to find a bath."

Standing as carefully as he might so he didn't end up like Titus, he reached for the top of the trench, trying to pretend he wasn't covered in shit from head to toe.

Titus had rolled over and glared at him, his eyes the lone spots of white in the gray-ish brown that coated Titus from head to toe.

Antonius didn't envy the man. He didn't look back as he climbed out of the latrine and went in search of a bath.

The camp bath would be the first place Titus went when he finally climbed out of that cursed shit hole, so Antonius avoided that. But he needed a bath, so badly. The muck was dripping everywhere. He knew of a small pond to the south, but that would mean marching his feces-covered self through the camp, and probably coming face-to-face with the guard commander, or worse.

He recalled from the days before that they had passed a few swampy ponds and even a slightly larger, clear lake as they marched north in the Caledonii lands, and the thought of cool, clean water was just what he needed. Breathing as sparsely as he could, he walked more eastward, then north toward the wall where the willow was. He flicked his head from left to right, checking the guards. This side of the wall was empty and unguarded. Soldiers were busy with their daily work and not watching the low-lying demarcation of the Caledonii lands.

They wouldn't be looking for a Roman solider, anyway. After all, what Roman was going to head north by himself?

Antonius slipped over the wall easily, the feces on his backside helping with that endeavor, and he paused to study the landscape. Straight north, if he recalled correctly, the veering east. They had marched through the trees, and he'd seen the water glinting in the pale sun. As he walked, he continued to breathe shallowly through his mouth to avoid smelling his rancid self.

It had to be here somewhere. . .

There it is!

Thank the Gods. The smell was starting to turn his stomach.

The glinting lake called to him like a siren, beckoning him to wash every spot and stain away.

He didn't pause to remove his shit-stained tunic. Instead, he marched straight into the clear, cool water, wading quickly until the water was at his chest where his crusty tunic clung as a second skin. Then he dove in, the blue-green waters thankfully washing away the first layer of muck.

When he resurfaced, he took a moment to gaze around at the small lake. Surrounded on two sides by brush and rock, the secluded pond was the perfect bathing spot. A decently tall waterfall erupted at where the rocks came together at the most northern part of the pond, splashing in a steady run, impossibly enticing. It was like something from a dream. Elysium on earth. Antonius swam toward the running water.

The water was shallower and clearer than the water by the grassy edge where he'd entered, and he took advantage of the rocks and crisp, pouring water to undress fully and stand naked under the falls. The water came to just below his hips and he reached under to scoop up a mix of sandy dirt and used it to scrub at every last crevice on his body. The prospect of any shit hiding caked in the bend of his knee or behind his ear made his stomach churn again.

He also rubbed the sandy dirt in his hair and rinsed it over and over in the falls, washing away any shit stuck in his hair. Cool though the water was, colder than he was used to, the refreshing water and air rivaled any Roman bath. He even filled his mouth and spat over and over to cleanse his palate until he couldn't taste that stench anymore.

Once most of the shit was gone, he tipped the crown of his head into the falls and inhaled deeply, clearing his lungs from the foetid stench just as he cleared it from his skin.

Never had air smelled or tasted so good.

Rubbing his face one final time, he left the rush of water and floated on his back, his face to the sky. It was the first time he'd had alone, truly alone, since he'd joined the army and come to this desolate place. And also, for the first time, listening to the lapping of the low waves against the rock and the vibrant chirping of the birds in the trees behind him, he enjoyed being in this strange land. There was a sense of calm and peace about it — the rustling of the leaves, the birdsong in his ears.

In fact, he just might —

"Are ye quite done lounging about? Other people would like their bath."

Antonius flipped over at the sound of the delicate voice chastising him. He wiped the dripping water from his eyes to see who had interrupted his bath. Not another soldier. The voice was too light for that.

Then who —?

He froze where he stood in the water at the woman before him.

It was the same woman from the day before.
Muireall.

He flicked his gaze to look behind her. She seemed to be alone.

"Are ye that soldier from a few days past? The one traipsing somewhere he shouldn't be? 'Twould seem that's a problem ye have, seeing as ye are somewhere ye shouldn't be today."

She stood by the rocks on the east side of the lake, her eyes leisurely roving over his exposed body, from his dripping head to the sharp bones of his hips and the planes of his belly that led to his cock, barely submerged under the water.

Antonius stood frozen, unsure of how to react. How did one respond to a red-headed barbarian when caught swimming naked in her lake?

He moved in the water, walking backward toward his sopping wet tunic. She leveled her gaze at him and pursed her lips as she watched him try to move away.

She reminded him of a mural he'd seen once in Rome, of the goddess Persephone, only with red hair instead of flaxen. Her buxom chest and wide hips were accented by the wide leather belt around her waist, cinched tight to keep her tunic-like dress in place. Her red curls, so wild they seemed to have their own life force, danced around her moonlight face and reached almost to her belt. Her eyes studied him like a predator watched its prey, and she held tight to a checkered blanket folded over her arm.

"Ye aren't thinking of running away, are ye? Report me to your leaders? Not as naked as the day ye were born?" A wisp of a smile crossed her full, deep pink lips.

Was she . . .was she *mocking* him?

A dimple on her cheek peeked in and out.

She *was!* She was *laughing* at him.

He finally reached his stained tunic, which looked and smelled only slightly better than it had moments ago, and draped it around his waist before stepping into shallower waters closer to her.

"I have a tunic, I'll have you know," he responded, hoping he hid enough from her. Her aggressive gaze, however, told him she was ardently looking. "And I didn't mean to intrude on your private lake. I'll give you leave."

He lifted a leg to step onto a rock and realized that, between holding the tunic and grabbing the rocks to balance as he stepped out, he was going to show her all he had to offer. And her eager eyes didn't move — she was waiting for him to do just that. He paused and turned to glare at her.

"If you don't mind?" he asked with emphasis. Why was she watching him?

Muireall's sly smile widened. "I don't mind at all."

Antonius frowned. Her response was not what he'd expected. Maybe he'd spoken the words wrong. But he lacked any other way of expressing himself. And now he was going to have to put his tunic back on as she watched with glee. With an inward groan, he lifted his semi-cleaned yet still-rank tunic over his head and grimaced as the cool fabric slid over his back. A low whistle carried over the lake. Antonius whipped around at the woman.

"Thank ye for that view, Roman. Now that ye have your vile clothing on, will ye please leave before I let our warriors know that, once again, ye've breached the wall?"

Dressed, he climbed up the rock and faced the woman who stood several steps away.

"My apologies, I fear I needed a bath —"

"I'll say." She wrinkled her nose at him. "What happened to ye? Is that —" She leaned in close to a stain and gave a quick sniff before recoiling. "Is that shite?" Her brow creased with the question.

"Shite?" he repeated.

"Shite? Dung?" She covered her nose with a hand. "What happened to ye?"

Antonius ran his hand through his damp hair. What was it about this brilliantly red woman that made him so flustered? He was a Roman Legionnaire, after all! One woman shouldn't have the ability to throw him off, no matter how comely the woman was. Or how her full breasts jiggled under the rounded neckline of her long tunic . . .

Focus, Antonius!

"Oh, I got into a fight."

Her smile curled like she knew what to make of that answer. "Where? In a mucking stall?"

He swept his eyes right and tipped his head to her. "You aren't far off."

"Weel, ye still stink. Or at least your léine does."

"My *léine*?" He leaned forward, trying to understand her thick brogue.

She picked at her own gown. "Your léine?"

"Oh, my tunic. Yes, I was wearing it in the fight."

"Are ye going to wear it back? Ye dinna bring another léine? And why are you here for a bath? Have ye no lochs in your camp?"

The rapid-fire questions threw him off again, and he had to take a moment to understand each one.

"Yes, I have no other clothing with me. No, I was too rushed to wash off the shite before I got here. And I didn't want to bathe at camp, because of the fight." Then he paused, and his eyes narrowed.

In his wet bluster, he'd forgotten the reason for the fight that had sent him here. The Prefect was looking for this very woman and her companions! What if he had been followed? It was dangerous for her to be near him . . .

"Are ye there?" she interrupted his thoughts.

He cast his gaze around the trees, searching for any sign of glinting shields or red tunics. Muireall caught his movement and scanned the trees as well, then landed back on him and pulled her checkered blanket against her chest.

"What is it? Is someone here?"

He shook his head. "No, but there could be. I don't think I was followed, but I can't be sure. It's dangerous —"

"Aye, dangerous for ye," she retorted, loosening her grip on her blanket.

Antonius shook his head again. "No, not for me. Well, I mean, yes, I know I'm on Caledonii land and I shouldn't be. But I'm only here to wash. I'm not here to attack or anything."

Muireall flipped her crimson curls over her shoulder. "Then what is the danger?"

Something inside him took control, moving him with an undeniable force that pressed him to step close to Muireall and stare down at her. She needed to take him seriously. He had a sudden urge to let her know what the danger was in detail. His fealty to his own army be damned.

"It's dangerous for you. For you and your companions. Yes, there's a treaty, but our Prefect isn't planning on abiding by it, and he wants to make an example of you and your friends."

"*Prefect*?" Her Latin was garbled, but he understood her confusion.

"Prefect. He's our military leader in this area, presiding over a few forts at the wall. He doesn't agree with the treaty and is looking for any chance to break it, show our high command we need to keep up aggressions and bring your people to heel."

He had reached out a hand, palm up, not to touch her but in supplication, a poor habit of his. She glanced down at his hand and shuffled backward, a moue of fear eliminating her easy smile as she narrowed her eyes.

"Why are you telling me all this?" she asked in a nervous voice. Her lighthearted nature was gone, replaced by fear, and he didn't blame her at all. "Ye are my enemy. Why would ye tell me all this? Is this a ploy to trick me? To trick the Caledonii?"

Antonius didn't know how a ploy to trick her might trick her entire tribe of people, but he didn't ask. And he couldn't answer the question of why very well himself. His sense of honor was dictating his words, and Antonius's primary concern was to quell her fears and perchance get a peek at another one of her smiles.

"No, no trick. Not from me. I don't agree with my Prefect. But my thoughts don't matter. I'm a lowly soldier, so I have to obey my commanders, whether I agree with them or not."

Her head snapped back at that. "What? Warriors can no' contradict their leaders? What poor leaders you must have, if men are no' free to speak their minds. What lousy, empty-headed decisions they must make, hearing only their own voices."

Antonius pursed his lips — Rome heard her own voice had fared pretty well. The Roman Army had brought most of the known world under its control at the command of that voice. But Muireall had a point. What might the army, and Rome, have accomplished if the leaders listened half as much as they spoke?

He reached out to her again. "Please, Muireall, listen to me. Warn your friends. I don't know what you were doing far from your village but have caution if you travel again. The Prefect's desires are the desires of my entire Centauriae. And I'd not have you fall to his sword over his own petty claims for power."

Her golden green eyes narrowed again, but she didn't step back. "How do you know my name?"

"Your friend, the one you called Gwyneth, she said it to you. At least, I assumed it was your name. My *Gaelig* is not as fine as it could be. That's your name, right? Muireall?"

She inclined her head slightly. "Aye. I'm called Muireall. But it does no' seem fair."

Antonius blinked rapidly. "What doesn't seem fair?"

Her smile came back — thanks be to the gods! — if only a small curl at the corner of her mouth.

"I dinna know your name."

Antonius dropped his head to hide his smile. He hadn't had many reasons to smile as of late, and the gesture felt almost foreign on his lips. Then he lifted his head again to her.

"Antonius. I am called Antonius."

She tried to say it several times, practicing the roll of it on her tongue. His name sounded rather long and magnanimous with the slow roll she added to it.

He wasn't sure if she realized it, but she had shifted forward as they spoke, and she was now close enough for him to twine a curl around his finger if he desired — *and oh, did he desire!* — but he dared not. It would not have been the least bit appropriate, no matter how much he wanted to.

"Why are ye helping me, and my people, like this, Antonius?" she asked. It was a hard question, but one to which he felt his simple, if unclear, answer was best.

"I was raised to do what you vow to do and not to break a promise. Our treaty with your people is a vow, and the Prefect wants to break that vow. It's not what men of honor do. Real men keep their word."

The answer sounded paltry and pathetic to his own ears. Muireall worked her lips, weighing Antonius's words. She must have believed him because she nodded, then reached out and patted his arm.

"I will take the chance to believe ye," she told him. "But what happens when ye return to your soldiers and they decide to attack or do something else to break the treaty? Is there anything my tribe can do?"

Antonius glanced around the secluded lake. It seemed as fine a place as any for subterfuge. Maybe he wouldn't get caught and executed for treason, meeting her here.

But weak as his words sounded, his words to Muireall were true. He couldn't, in good faith, follow through with orders that broke a treaty signed by the very empire he served. He was a better man than that.

"We can meet here. Alone preferably. By myself on your land, I'm at far more of a disadvantage than you are."

"How will we know when to meet? I can check here throughout the day, but ye can't."

"How about this? I can probably sneak out at night after the camp beds down for the night. If there is something to worry about, I can leave a sign. I'll tie off a piece of this to that willow there." He gripped the stained tunic as he pointed. He certainly wouldn't be wearing it again after his shit-fight. "Then meet me the next night, and I will let you know what I've heard."

She nodded. "Aye, this loch is rather remote. Our village is no' too close. Another loch is closer to the north, but I prefer the privacy of this one."

He gave her a tight smile. "Then we are of the same mind. So will this place work? Will that plan suffice?"

"What if I have to send a message to you?" she asked.

Antonius couldn't image her need to send him a message, but the reverse process should work.

"Then leave me a piece of fabric. I don't know if I can come every night after nightfall, but I'll try."

This time when she reached for his arm, she squeezed it gently, and his entire body lit afire at her touch.

"I dinna fully understand why ye would go against your own people, Antonius, but I thank ye for it." She dropped his arm and stepped back quickly, as if she'd been caught doing something wrong. "Ye should leave now. I've been gone a fair time, as have ye, and we will both be missed. And I still must bathe."

Antonius bowed formally from the waist, then stepped past her, heading south toward the wall.

He forced himself not to look back to watch her bathe. He wanted desperately to lay his eyes upon that bare, moonlit skin as she crested through the water.

But she'd come to that lake for privacy, and privacy he'd give her.

The Roman of the North

Chapter Five: Gossip and Rumors

    Muireall's skin fairly shimmered as she walked back to Kilsyth from her bath, a needed respite for such a warm day. Though the water may have cooled her skin, it did nothing for her fevered brain.

    She hadn't expected to find anyone at the loch, what with the village busy with summer chores and taking advantage of the dry, bright day. She had finished her work early and snuck away from her parents, knowing the loch would be empty. At least it was *supposed* to be empty.

    Discovering a naked Roman in the water was the last thing she expected. Hadn't he learned his lesson about staying off Caledonii land?

    But her desire to school him in his error was overpowered by her desire to enjoy the vision he presented. Swimming on his back, he'd cut through the water like fire through quartz, his sun-kissed skin dripping as his finely honed muscles worked. His black cropped hair beaded in the water, while the darker patches of hair scattered across his chest and down to his manhood that laid nearly to his jutting hip bone.

    Muireall had to bite her hand at the sight of him. Not as tall as most of the Caledonii men, but respectfully broad enough with sharp and powerful definition in every muscle. Being a Roman soldier carved him as if from stone, and Muireall's deep and resounding reaction to his naked body kept her riveted on his not-so-private swim. She'd found him attractive enough whilst in the woods, at least for an odd Roman soldier, but to see his body, one blessed by the gods . . .

    What might it be like to take that body to her bed, between her legs? He might not be overly tall, but his cock was more than enticing enough. . . .

    Then she had shaken her head, clearing it from such thoughts. What had she been thinking? He was a Roman soldier, an invader in her land, her *enemy*! This was not a man to be trusted, let alone brought to her bed. He was the last person who should find himself between her thighs.

    Yet, when he'd encountered them in the thicket of trees, he'd let them go, albeit at Gwyneth's sword point, and hadn't reported them to his fellow soldiers, which he easily could have done. Why had he agreed to let them escape?

    And then when she approached him at the loch — what had possessed her? He was right about the danger. And to agree on a method of communication with the man?

    Ooch, the goddess was playing with her for certain.

    On her walk home, no matter how many times she scolded herself that he was a Roman, the softness of his skin and the intensity of his glittering dark eyes kept flitting through her head as a captivating reminder of her reaction to him, of her foolish interest.

    While she wanted to keep her interlude with Antonius private, as private as the loch had been, Muireall felt she would explode unless she shared her encounter with someone. It would have to be Gwyneth — no one else yet knew of their chance meeting with the soldier from the day before, at least as far as Muireall knew, unless Gwyneth told her father, which she might have done. Gwyneth might be rough and tumble, more comfortable with a bow or sword than children or sewing, but she was a fiery woman nonetheless. She'd report Roman movements on Caledonii land.

She'd also understand Muireall's reaction, and perhaps help her counter it.

Nothing good could come of pining for a Roman.

Muireall had lingered in both her bath and walk home, and by the time she entered the open village gate, the shadows were long on the grass, and scents of mutton and roasted vegetables welcomed her. A lamb trotted up, having escaped from its pen and braying mam, and nuzzled her palm. She stroked its soft, downy fleece that was starting to sprout and returned it to its pen, where it jumped joyfully to its mother.

"I've been trying to fix the pens all day," a voice to her right called out, causing her to jump under her skin. Evan had been bent over, and she only noticed him now that he stood up and spoke. His light brown hair was woven with straw and wood dust, and it sprinkled across his cheeks like bright freckles.

"Ooch, Evan, I did no' see ye there! Are ye working today? How's the ankle?"

He peered down at his own leg, the one he'd twisted in the woods with her and Gwyneth, and lifted it to show her the binding around his lower leg. Gwyneth's sister, Ayla, possessed a skillful hand at the healing arts, and she seemed to have taken care of the wound.

"It aches if I put too much weight on it, but Aila said I might still work as long as I could sit or rest it. I can stand just fine on my other leg, so I'm resting my knee on this stump. I just move the stump as I move around the pen. But these wily lambs are finding every weak plank before I can fix them."

Evan sent an accusatory glare at said lambs bounding and braying in play. Muireall smiled at the wee beasties.

"And none of your brothers came to aid ye?" Muireall flicked her gaze around the lambing pens.

Evan shook his head. "Nay. Eian is off on some errand for the chieftain, and I dinna know what Edan is up to. Nay good, if I know him."

Muireall giggled lightly. "Aye, that I can see. Have ye seen Gwyneth? I'd like to speak with her."

Evan's face darkened, his pale blue eyes hooded. "About what happened in the grove?"

Muireall stilled, trying not to react. Best he not know she'd just met that very soldier they'd threatened in the forest.

"Nay. Why? Have ye heard more about it? Did Gwyneth share our encounter with her father?"

Evan dipped his head. "No' that I know. The warriors haven't moved toward any action, and none in the village appears concerned, so I'd wager no. But if they dinna think the threat is a real one, then they'd have the same reaction."

Muireall inhaled deeply, not sure why a sense of relief washed over her. "Weel, then. I best be off. Enjoy your misbehavin' lambs!" Muireall kept her voice cheery as she walked off, heading toward the chieftain's wide wheelhouse.

Muireall had spent much of her youth in and around the chieftain's wheelhouse as she played with Gwyneth and her younger sister Sloane. As they had grown, duties and chores took up more of their time, but she and Gwyneth had always remained close, though many considered them opposites.

Muireall was shorter, with a fuller frame, unruly curly hair, and a light-hearted charm that made her beloved in the village. The younger sister in her small family, she had a wild imagination that oft got her and Gwyneth in trouble.

Gwyneth, however, was the longer version of Muireall — longer, sunset-red hair that fell in waves more than curls that she tied back with a leather thong most days, a longer frame that made her as tall as her sisters and nearly as tall as her own father, the mighty chieftain Ru Blogh. And she was more serious when it came to her interests and skills — archery, tracking, swordplay — skills only a few women in the village took more seriously. While all the women in the village could carry their weight in a fight, Gwyneth was the only one who could easily take on a well-armed man, or two, and vanquish them with ease.

Instead of entering the chieftain's wheelhouse, Muireall followed the patchy grass to the rear, where she knew she'd find Gwyneth using her practice target or attacking a wooden dummy with her training sword. From the quiet that welcomed her, Muireall guessed it was the former. She was right.

Gwyneth stood tall and proud in her light gray *léine*, her body angled so her arm extended straight at the target. Her mass of amber hair was tied in a loose tail and hung halfway down her back. She was a vision of the warrior goddess Morrigan herself. Then she loosed the arrow, and with a subdued thunk, the arrow struck its mark, just a smidgen off-center.

"*Mhac Na Galla.*"

Muireall smiled at Gwyneth's under-her-breath curse. Out of respect, Muireall cleared her throat lightly to interrupt her friend.

Gwyneth barely turned her head as she reset her bow with another arrow from the quiver resting near her feet.

"Muireall. How nice of ye to finally join us. Dinna think I didn't see ye sneak off, and from the looks of your damp hair, I presume ye found your bath?"

Gwyneth lifted the bow with a precise move of her arm, took aim, and shot again, this time striking dead center. A twitch of a smile tugged at her lips. Muireall grinned widely at her friend.

"Nice shot."

Gwyneth dropped her bow arm and swiveled to face Muireall. "Dinna change the subject, *mo cara.* Did ye enjoy your bath? Are ye now here to flaunt it before me?"

"Ooch, says the woman who spent her day with her weapons rather than in her house cooking or cleaning?" Muireall countered.

Gwyneth's cheeks pinked, and a slight smile grew on her face.

"Ye've got me on that one. We are a pair of layabouts, we are." Gwyneth set her bow against her quiver, then squinted at Muireall. "But mayhap ye have more to tell than just how cool the water was?"

Muireall dropped her gaze to her skirts, finding the creamy, flint-colored flax more interesting. Gwyneth's mouth fell open.

"What happened at the loch? I can tell ye are hiding something from me." Gwyneth leaned in close, dwarfing Muireall under the inquisitive stare.

"Nay, I mean, naught happened. No' really," Muireall sputtered. *Oh, how did Gwyneth read her so well?* And why was she suddenly so unsettled at her meeting with Antonius? It's not like she did anything untoward with him.

Yet, she had wanted to. What if Gwyneth could see that as plainly as the nose on her face? They'd been friends since they were lassies. She probably *could* read it on her face.

One sleek, strawberry-blonde eyebrow rose on Gwyneth's face. "No' really?"

Muireall licked her lips. "I was no' quite alone at the loch."

Gwyneth's other eyebrow joined the first. "Och, ye weren't, were ye? Who did ye meet there?"

"Ye recall the Roman from the grove?"

Gwyneth's comical leering stopped, and she stiffened upright, her eyes narrow. "Aye. I recall the man. Tell me he did no' breach the wall again."

"Did ye tell your father about the first time?"

Gwyneth shook her head before shifting her gaze to the clear pink and gray horizon. "I told him we saw Roman soldiers in the glen, but not of our meeting one in the woods. Father would have lost his mind if such a thing happened. He's already lost one daughter in marriage to a Roman. I didn't want him to fret losing another. I dinna think he finds the Romans much of a threat. They've ventured on this side of the *cnap-starra* wall."

Muireall didn't respond, and Gwyneth's eyes came back to her with understanding. "He was at the loch? What was he doing there? Was he looking for our village?" Her voice rose as she spoke, and Muireall waved her hand at Gwyneth. She didn't want Gwyneth to worry over nothing. And it was *nothing*.

"Nay, he wasn't looking for anything. He was, well, bathing."

"Bathing? Why was he bathing in our loch?"

"From what I could see, 'twas to wash shite from his skin after a fight."

"What manner of warrior gets covered in shite in a fight? And why did he no' bathe at his camp?"

So many questions! Muireall gave Gwyneth a half-shrug. "I'm no' sure exactly how he became covered in shite.

He mentioned he fought with a man at the place where they release their bowels, and he didn't want his fellow soldiers to know."

"Ye spoke to him?" Gwyneth asked in a harsh whisper, grabbing Muireall's arm in a painful grip. "What possessed ye? He might have slain ye were ye stood?"

With what? Muireall bit at the inside of her cheek to hold back a smile. She didn't want to irritate her worried friend, but she was unsuccessful.

"What? Why do ye grin so? Ye should take this seriously, Muireall! What if he'd had a weapon on ye?"

At this, Muireall burst out laughing. He'd only had one weapon, and it wasn't one that might slay her, but 'twas one she wouldn't mind having stab her over and over.

"Muireall! What ails ye?"

Muireall coughed into her hand, trying to regain herself. "Och, Gwyneth, 'tis no' as ye think. He had no weapon on him, no' as ye think. He had no clothes to speak of."

The look of shock on Gwyneth's face flashed but a moment, before her features softened and a sly grin pulled up her lips to one side. Her grip on Muireall became light.

"Oh, ye found him in the middle of *his* bath. Right, and in a state of undress, I presume?" Unlike Muireall, Gwyneth didn't try to hide her smile.

"Gwyneth!" *Och, her friend could read her too well!*

"Mayhap that's why he was so forthcoming with information. But why come to the loch where ye like to bathe? 'Tis rather private. The whole reason ye bathe there, if I recall ye correctly."

Muireall nodded and averted her eyes. "'Twas more than that. And that's why I sought ye out. Ye may want to tell your father that the Romans have nefarious intentions, mayhap even ones that will break our treaty, according to this Antonius.

They are doing more than wandering north of the wall. He sought to warn me."

"Antonius, eh?" Gwyneth's voice was heavy with implication as she smirked.

"Aye. He appeared to be a man of honor. He said he does no' agree with breaking the treaty."

Gwyneth's bright green eyes narrowed again. "Roman movements? Aye, I shall have to figure out a way to tell father of this. And I'll do my best to keep ye out of it." Gwyneth crossed her long, toned arms across her chest. "He sure was eager to share an abundance of information, enemy information, with ye. Recall who this man is, what side he fights for. It might be a trick."

Muireall felt the heat rise from her neck to her cheeks. "Aye, that he did. I know he is my enemy, and I'm no' about to trust my enemy. I said the same to him, and he vowed 'twas otherwise. He seemed earnest, so I dinna believe it to be a trick. Yet, I dinna know why he was so eager to share so much with me."

Gwyneth's eyes moved up and down Muireall's curvaceous form. "Och, don't ye now?" She grinned. Muireall swatted at her. "Was he at least worth looking at? He's a warrior, a Roman, aye, but they train for hours, I've heard. So?"

Muireall squinted at Gwyneth. "So, what?"

"So was he worth it, the risk of a Roman at your private bath?"

Muireall's cheeks were on fire.

"Aye, he was worth it."

Gwyneth must have spoken to her father right away. Not that Muireall blamed her, because the next day was not one of busy chores and jovial villagers. Mother kept their children near the center hearth of their wheelhouses and their axes and swords by the door. Trick or no, well-armed warriors patrolled the wall and guarded the gate, both inside and out. Evan had his spear in hand and his leg resting on his stump near the gate, ready to attack even with an injured ankle. Muireall could only imagine what Ayla would have to say about *that*.

The problem was, she had told Antonius she'd return to the loch to check for his knotted fabric message, and she'd never get past the guards. What he if left a piece of tunic and wanted to meet her the next night, and she missed it? A poor method of communication, true, but the only one they had.

Gwyneth might have been able to help her sneak past the guards. And the chieftain's daughter was nearly as strong with her bow as any of the warriors, so Muireall wouldn't have to worry for her safety. But as the chieftain's daughter, the warriors would never permit Gwyneth out of the village with the threat of Romans nearby, no matter her fighting skills.

So having Gwyneth aid her was out.

Though she wasn't sure why she kept it a secret, Muireall also hadn't mentioned to her friend that she planned on meeting the Roman again. So asking Gwyneth was not a wise idea, to be sure.

Her best chance was to try to sneak out at dusk, mayhap find a distraction, then sneak back once she checked the loch.

Muireall sighed as she stared at the gate from the stone edge of the well. What manner of distraction might turn the guards from their duty and permit her to slip out?

She yanked the pail to the edge, refocusing on her task. Any message Antonius would send might have to wait a day or two.

But what good was that? The whole point behind the communication was to help her village in case of an attack — and here her warriors were, preventing that very thing.

The water in the pail sloshed at her absent-minded movements, spilling on her thin leather shoes.

"Ballocks," she muttered under her breath, wiping her feet against her skirts.

Just another thing she didn't need this day.

The Roman of the North

Chapter Six: Information

After his fight with Titus, Antonius kept his head down and his words to himself. He wasn't seen as much of a talker anyway, so it made it easy for him to fall off the Prefect's radar and for his fellow Centauriae to ignore him.

Titus didn't even look his way all the next day, which suited Antonius fine. Cassius, however, had no such compunctions, and marched next to him on drills. The guard commander was working them hard, and Antonius was certain the intensity of the drills meant something big on the horizon. He had to figure out a way to slip out and warn Muireall. And perchance meet with the ripened, wild haired woman . . .

"What do you think they're planning?" Cassius interrupted Antonius's thoughts. Antonius flicked his eyes toward Cassius and tried to cover his distracted thoughts.

"What?"

Cassius tipped his chin at the guard commander. "The commanders. The Prefect. What do you think they're planning?

Why all this hard training today? And I don't see them stopping anytime soon. Are there hostilities with the barbarians? Did the Prefect say anything to you?"

Antonius worked his jaw as he considered Cassius's questions. He'd been trying to find out the same, and it seemed Cassius had more information than Antonius.

"Why? Is there something you've heard?" Better to turn the question around on him, learn if Cassius knew anything.

"Only that the Prefect has a distinct dislike for these Caledonii, but you know that. We all do. And rumors have started that he's not content to leave the treaty be. Didius sees it as weak, from what the legionnaires say. He, like most of the Legion, *hates* these barbarians. If he can't find a valid reason to invade, he'll create one, that I do know." Cassius rambled off his thoughts, just one soldier gossiping to another.

"So, encountering some Caledonii when we were on the wrong side of the wall is a valid reason to break the treaty?" Antonius inquired.

The excuse seemed too weak to be plausible. It lacked honor. Did Cassius believe the same?

Cassius shrugged under his heavy plated armor. "Well, if they attack first, he doesn't care what side of the wall he's on. But I thought you might have heard something more specific, like when the attack will be. Since you are tight with Titus."

At this, Antonius broke formation and turned his head to Cassius. "Tight with Titus?"

Cassius nodded, sweat dripping from the sides of his face and staining his red neck scarf a deep russet brown. "I saw you with him yesterday. He's been tight-lipped but —"

"No, I'm not tight with Titus."

"Well, I'd rather you were. Then you might know what's going on." Cassius shifted his attention back to the lead formation. He didn't want to risk getting caught out of formation by his commander, and Antonius followed his move. Getting caught would mean more punishment, and Antonius had already had enough of digging latrines to last a lifetime. He was certain he still caught whiffs of muck and waste when the breeze caught his nose the right way.

They fell silent, focusing on their formation, their marching near the wall. But Antonius's attention wasn't on the formation.

No, it was on Titus, who marched nearer the front of the formation, and on how he might find out what Titus knew about the Prefect's plans to break the treaty.

That night, after hours of marching and practicing different iterations of their powerful shield wall so much they could barely lift their arms over their heads, most men fell into bed right after the evening meal. Sunrise would rear its bright head early, and the soldiers needed as much time as they might find to recover from the brutal work of the day.

The lamp in Androdinus's tent gave off an incandescent glow in the early evening, giving Antonius enough light to move by. He had followed Titus there and found a space near the tent where he could see Titus and Androdinus's dark outline and hear them speak. If they decided to discuss the Prefect's orders, which Titus would — the man had no ability to hold his tongue — Antonius wanted to hear it.

Antonius's entire body ached from his chin to the soles of his feet, but he ignored the screaming in his muscles and crouched by the rear of the tent, hiding in the shadows. Titus and Androdinus spoke in low tones, and if everyone else in the camp hadn't already been asleep, Antonius never would have heard them.

But Titus was a loudmouth too, and the more he spoke, the more impassioned and louder he got.

Fool, Antonius thought.

They didn't discuss the Prefect's obsession with the Caledonii right away. Rather, they shared notes on which moves had brought more women to his bed and in what way.

Fools, he thought again. Androdinus had struck Antonius as a man who was guided by his cock, and it seems Antonius was correct.

His head dropped between his knees as they droned on, and his eyes drooped. He might have even started to doze when Titus's voice cut through his hazy sleepiness.

"The Prefect wants small cohorts of men, two or three at most, on the other side of the wall, daily. At least along our stretch of the wall, since we appear to be closest to some of the major villages."

Antonius's head snapped up at the word *Prefect*, and he leaned in silently, wiping the sleep from his eyes as he listened to Titus's next words.

"What are we to do whilst there?" Androdinus asked. Antonius imagined him on the edge of his pallet, hanging onto Titus's every word.

"We are to find lone Caledonii, those hunting or walking between villages. Preferably those with weapons who might fight back. We are to capture them if we can, kill them if not, and bring them back to camp as evidence of the Caledonii breaking the treaty. Then Didius can request Emperor Severus abandon the treaty and invade, quelling these wild barbarians once and for all."

Antonius found it difficult to breathe. His chest clenched at Titus's ease with such deception, and the Prefect's encouraging it. What was it with these men of power that they might set aside a treaty made in good faith? What was the value of such a vow, then? And why did some men find the need to win at all costs?

It was as bad as he'd thought.

He shook his head and slid away from the tent before creeping back to his own.

The Roman of the North

Chapter Seven: Drunkards

  Titus might not return to the tent at all, if he and Androdinus plotted through the night. His other tent-mate snored like an ox, so Antonius had no worries that the man would sleep through any wayward sounds of his rummaging through his belongings. His hand landed on the very item he was searching for — a rough strip of woolen fabric, much like the one he used a few nights before…
  Clutching it tight in his fist, Antonius arranged his blankets so it might look like he was yet in bed, threw a quick glance over his shoulder at his oblivious tent-mate, then rushed from his tent into the star-lit night.
  A rounding half-moon hung in the sky, barely enough light to see by, but better to hide his escape over the crumbling wall at the willow tree. Antonius slipped into the night without raising alarm, and he grimaced as he walked. What did such lack of security and guard mean about the Roman army this far north? Were they getting lazy, or did they just no longer care about the Caledonii's threat? Or was the Prefect hoping a few

young Caledonii might sneak over the wall and attack, thus justifying his breaking the treaty? Either way, the lack of guards lent credibility to the Prefect's bloodthirsty desires for conquest.

Finding the lake would be more difficult under the heavy blanket of darkness, but Antonius had made sure to note certain markers — odd stone shapes or bent tree limbs — when he'd returned the day before. He wanted to be prepared for this very type of occurrence.

The trek took longer than he liked, but when he cut through the final copse of trees at the black pool that reflected the half-moon with a light sparkle, Antonius's chest relaxed. Searching the dark perimeter, he finally landed on the spot he believed would be best for Muireall to see his message. The oak was tall, and sturdy branches extended low on the trunk — the perfect place to tie off his scrap of wool. Bright red during the day, it should contrast against the greens and browns of the trees to be readily visible.

Antonius tugged on the ends of the fabric, making sure it was tight. He didn't want it to loosen and blow away, the gods forbid. His mind went to the maid he hoped would see it, her thick hair and lush body . . . and then cursed his own thoughts. Was he trying to save her people or were his intentions much less noble?

He rubbed at his face with his bare hand and gave the red signal a final appraisal.

It didn't matter if he did it because he wanted the woman or because he wanted to aid his enemy.

He was risking his own life to send a message, and if she got that message, that was all that mattered.

At least, that's what he told himself as he marched back to his camp in the darkness.

Sunset the following day came quickly for Antonius, who struggled to keep his mind on his work and his field practice. It kept drifting to that flapping scrap of fabric and the woman who needed to find it.

Another day of heavy lifting, marching, and this time added sword and spear practice meant another weary night for the lowly legionnaires. Only this night, while many found their beds early, others decided to drink the night away instead. Antonius clenched his jaw as he scanned the soldiers milling about with flagons of pilfered ale and loud, raucous voices. Most stripped down to naught but waist clothes as they tried to cool themselves from the hot training of the day, and finding their tents was not high on their list of priorities.

Why did they select this night for drunken celebration? He had to sneak away. If the festivities stayed to the south of the camp, maybe he could . . .

A slap on the back shocked Antonius into awareness and as he flinched, he looked over his shoulder at the solidly build man grinning behind him. Cassius, also naked but for a swath of linen around his hips, held out a skin of throat-burning wine, offering Antonius a drink.

Against his better judgment, Antonius smiled back and took the proffered wine. Better to get Cassius well and truly drunk so he might leave unnoticed for the wall. He might avoid Titus's angry glares as well, though he hadn't seen where the man went after supper. How long would Muireall wait? Antonius's eyes shifted to the moon as he drank deeply of the skin, choking the rough, dry liquid down. Not long enough, if he wanted to slip past his drunk mates.

"I was wondering if you were going to let go of your standards and drink with us lowly men," Cassius teased, his words slurring slightly. Antonius took that as good news. If he was already on the way to being into his cups, then Antonius might not have to help him along too much.

"I won't get as drunk as you are, you old vole, but I'll not turn down an offer of drink." Antonius tried to sound lighthearted back. He didn't want his heavy thoughts to be discovered.

Or anything else to be discovered.

Cassius slapped him again and grabbed his upper arm, dragging him past the tents, thankfully to the southern edge of the encampment. Three other men sat round a fire, sharing skins of wine and ale and sharing stories of their prowess to see who was the strongest or most brave. Androdinus sat in between two men while Antonius sat back a bit. If they all got drunk enough, the soldier might not notice if and when he left. And Cassius could tell them Antonius didn't drink or carouse, and they'd not care why he left.

A sound enough plan.

As long as they got very dunk, and fast.

Chapter Eight: Urgent Encounters

Their road to drunkenness was fast, faster than Antonius imagined — they must have been well into their cups before Antonius even joined them. They were singing a chant off-key when Antonius slipped away into the shadows and crept over the wall.

The trail was easier to follow this night. The moonlight had brightened over the past few days, and it would be a full moon soon. He was also learning his surroundings, becoming more familiar with the trees and hills and brush. Keeping his mind on his intentions, he ran toward the lake. What if it was too late? What if Muireall had given up waiting for him and left? They hadn't set any parameters for how long to wait for the other. What would happen to her and her village then?

The urgency in his message pushed his aching legs to the limit. He had to make it there before she left.

He *had* to.

Antonius burst through the trees to the lake, its crystalline black majesty glittering in the dappled moonlight. He worked his way toward the oak. Muireall was nowhere to be found.

He was too late.

His red fabric flapped limply against the oak, and Antonius rested his hand against the trunk and leaned his weary head on the cool bark. It had been a foolish plan to begin with.

A crunch of a stick cracked behind him.

Before he turned around, Antonius had the sudden, sickening thought that mayhap Muireall wouldn't return alone, that she didn't trust him and would bring her companions, or worse, several warriors with her. What reason did she have to trust him, truly, when he'd already told her that his army wanted to use them, use her, as a reason to re-invade Caledonii lands? That news didn't inspire confidence in one's enemy.

He spun around to see Muireall emerge from the brush behind him, a red sun on a dark night.

"You came," he said in a quiet rush of relief.

Muireall nodded but remained where she was by the brush, just beyond arm's reach.

"What did ye send the signal for? My village is on edge. My friend, Gwyneth, had to tell her father about the warning ye gave me."

"I'm not surprised. I'd be on edge as well. I'm rather surprised ye came alone."

A light breeze kicked up, flicking her hair around her head as she tugged at the sleeves of her tunic that was the color of the Roman sand. If she seemed nervous at meeting him alone, she didn't show it.

"Has something happened? Is that why ye left the signal?"

Antonius took an unconscious step closer to her, as if trying to guard her from the Roman soldiers to the south.

"I overheard a rumor about my Prefect. He's intent on breaking the treaty, and he plans on using our meeting in the glen to do it."

"Our meeting?" Her eyebrows flew up at his words, and he shook his head.

"No, my apologies, not where I met your companions and you. No one in my legion knows of *that* meeting. Rather, when our Centauriae breached the wall and saw you three from across the glen. He's going to claim your people attacked us, even though we were in the wrong in regards to the treaty. He will plead to our Legate to void the treaty and move on your people."

"Can he do that if your King committed to it? 'Tis treasonous, aye? Why would he do such a thing? And do ye know when? Or how?"

Antonius shrugged one shoulder, hating his dearth of information. "Why? Power, or recognition, most likely. For some men, once they get a taste of power, they are addicted."

"Addicted?" She repeated the word with a slow roll. He hadn't realized he'd said the word in Latin. He didn't know the word for it in her *Gaelig*.

"Consumed? They must have more?" She nodded, showing she understood, and waved him on to continue. "The when, that I do not know. Within days, perchance?"

Her pale face somehow lost even more color. "Days?"

He stepped closer and rested his hand on her sleeve. "I don't know for certain."

"Why should I trust you?" she asked suddenly.

Antonius snapped his head back. "What? Seems odd that you would ask that now, upon our third meeting."

Muireall pulled her shoulders tight and stared at him with hard eyes. "Ye are a Roman, the sworn enemy of my people. Ye are on Caledonii ground, breaking the treaty yourself. Ye've done that several times now. How do I know ye aren't here to trick me? To placate me whilst your soldiers march toward my home?"

Antonius froze. "What? What would it do for me to lie to you like that?"

"I dinna know! Mayhap this power ye speak of? Ye Romans, ye lie! And now your soldiers want to capture me and what? Sell me into slavery? Execute me?"

Her words broke his trance, and he lunged forward, grabbing her upper arms as she started to back away.

"No! Never! I'm a man of honor and would never want such a thing! I'm trying to save you —"

His fingers gripped her arms harder than he intended, but she still yanked, trying to wrest herself from his grasp.

"Why? Why would ye do that? Why do ye care about a barbarian Caledonii like me?" she screeched as she fought.

Antonius bent his elbows, slamming her against him. Hard.

"I thought it would be obvious," he told her in a growling voice before crushing his lips against hers.

Instead of struggling to get away, she stiffened slightly before softening, melting into the solid wall of his chest. His arms snaked around her back, holding her tightly against him as his tongue pressed forward, breaching the tender skin of her lips. She didn't yank her head back, but parted her lips, welcoming his tongue and sucked on it lightly.

He groaned his response. It may have been a while since he'd lain with a woman, but not so long to justify his reaction to *this* woman.

All he knew was the longer he kissed her, the more he wanted her. His cock twitched then throbbed, as if answering that call, pressing his warm length against her hip.

Muireall released his tongue and slipped her lips away from his. Her intense eyes looked up at his face.

"What do ye mean, Antonius? What is this?"

Antonius leaned his head down so his lips were a breath from hers. "I don't know what this is. All I know is from the moment your friend held me at sword point in the trees, I haven't been able to get you from my thoughts. And I would sooner put my own life at risk than see any soldiers get their hands on you."

"Risk your life?" she asked as she placed the palms of her hands flat on his panting chest.

"This moment right here could kill me," he whispered harshly. "I'd be executed as a traitor without question, without being able to plead my case, for aiding the enemy."

"Is that what I am? Your enemy?" Muireall asked, moving one of her hands from his chest to cup his jaw.

Antonius shook his head slightly. "Not my enemy. Rome's. But I'd sooner find my own death at the end of a Roman blade than see you subjected to the fevered whims of a man on a quest for power."

Then he paused and covered Muireall's hand on his chest with his own larger one and nuzzled her hand that cupped his face.

"But what of you? If you don't feel the same, I understand —"

He couldn't finish the rest. Muireall rose up on her toes and silenced him with a forceful kiss, one that demanded and commanded, and Antonius didn't fight it. He knew he was at her mercy. He'd been under her spell since that first moment in the trees.

He pressed her backward, holding her gently as he settled her into the damp grass. With only the moonlight reflecting on the lake as their light, and the gentle sound of lapping as their music, his hands moved up and down her body, grasping and grabbing at the material of her gown, trying to touch as much of her at once as he could.

Her legs shifted, spreading to allow his access to her pale thighs rivaled the hue of the moon. Smooth and beckoning, and he caressed his hand down her hip to where the hem of her skirts fell to expose her flesh to him. Her flesh that he couldn't get enough of.

His insides roiled, his cock demanding him to press forward and claim her as his own as his brain scolded him to slow down and savor each moment with her.

His fingers slipped to the side of her legs, to her tender skin leading to the darkly curled hairs guarding the entrance to her sheath. Antonius's manhood throbbed painfully, begging and searching, but he breathed out, forcing himself to go slow.

He might be ready to drive himself home, and though she was writhing and moaning under his kisses, that didn't mean she was ready.

With a deep groan rolling up from deep in his chest, he probed her with one finger, inserting it gently between the damp folds between her legs. She moaned and arched her back and grabbed at his head, holding him in place as their lips slanted and sucked, drinking from each other as if they'd both been in a drought, and only their kisses would revive them, give them life.

She moaned into his mouth when his finger entered her fully, and with his thumb, he flicked it artfully over the bud between her lower lips. Muireall yanked her head back and gasped at his touch.

"Antonius!" she whispered in a wavering voice. His head pounded and his cock throbbed and pulled. He wouldn't last much longer.

"I'll have you," he told her, shifting his face close to her ear. Her nimbus-like hair tickled his cheeks, making this moment between them somehow more tangible, more real. "I'll have you as mine, but not before you rise to your moment. I want you to rise higher than you ever have before."

Her fingertips curled in his hair, twining at the same pace as his thumb on her feminine bud. Her moans floated past his ears into the air, drowning out any sounds from the grass or lake. Muireall and her body, her reaction to the work of his fingers on her body, drowned out everything else.

They were drowning, drowning in each other.

Just when he thought his balls might explode if he didn't take her, she threw her head back again into the grass and gave out a high-pitched breath against his face. He slowed his thumb as he gazed at her face, noting every line of her eyes, the curve of her cheeks to her jaw, the reddish tinge of her eyebrows visible even in the dim light. Then one eye parted in a narrow slit. She reached down to grab his hand where his finger was still moving inside her and withdrew it from her sheath. His hand shined with the reflection from her juices.

"I want more than your finger," she cooed at him.

His body stiffened as his arm clenched around her, pressing them together.

"What do you want from me?" he asked in a heady pant. She could have asked for anything, the stars from the sky, the moon itself, and he would have wrestled the night to bring them to her.

"I want you," she answered simply, her hand slipping from his hand, down his chest to his cock, where she gripped it.

"It's yours. And when I take you and make you mine, you will be mine alone," he told her as he stared into her half-closed eyes. "I won't share you at all. And I'll tear down anyone who tries to keep me from you."

She gave him a scarce nod, and with that, he covered her fully, his hips fitting against hers as if they had been sculpted to fit, and his cock moved between her open, quivering thighs. But he didn't enter her, not right away.

He was poised at her opening, and she shifted under him, wrapping her legs around his hips to urge him on.

That was the only urging he needed.

He thrust between her legs, her warm sheath at once welcoming and pulsing, sucking him in. Muireall cast her head back with a gasp as he emitted a low, animalistic groan. When was the last time he'd lain with a woman? Years?

More importantly, when had he ever felt such passion? Such utter craving and need that made him dive into her again and again? Never.

Muireall was everything soft and enticing, and her mewling cries as his hips moved drove his need ever higher. He ground into her, his manhood pulsing to match the movement of her hips, and the harder he thrust, the more he needed her. He couldn't get deep enough.

In a heated mix of their grunting and groaning, a nearly painful stirring began deep in his loins, one that would not be denied.

If his life depended on it, he couldn't have stopped his crazed thrusting. Muireall's fingernails tore at his shoulders, urging him on, until their shared panting was the only sound either of them heard.

Then an explosion erupted from inside him and spewed out, and he stiffened above her with a final spine-tingling groan. And he was done, his seed spilled inside her and his need spent with it.

Yet he still couldn't move. Cracking his eyes open, he stared down at her face, a damp sheen of sweat making her skin appear even brighter in the moonlight, her eyes closed and a smile of ease and contentment upon her lips.

One of her fair eyes peeked open, and her smile widened as she returned his gaze. As he leaned down to kiss that smile, his moment of bliss was abruptly disturbed by one harrowing thought.

What had they done?

"This is dangerous." Muireall's voice was low and breathy against his face. She inhaled his uniquely Antonius scent — one of salt and work and his own musk. "No' just for ye, but for me. If anything happens, I'll be seen as a traitor to my people. That I somehow gave ye information about our tribes."

Antonius nuzzled his face into the damp curve of her neck, licking at her salty goodness. "Do you regret this? I'll leave, if so, and never invade on your life again, if you so desire."

The words bit at her like a wolf at its kill. Did he want to leave her now that he had her? She was foolish to believe it was anything more.

But to hope, to imagine . . .

"But that would kill me as soon much as the Roman army would," he continued.

Her hands dropped down under his tunic, and he shivered as she ran her fingertips up his backside.

"So ye are willing to risk your life for a roll in the grass?" Muireall teased lightly, trying to ignore the heavy implications of sleeping with the Caledonii enemy. That thought added too much weight to what they'd just shared, and she didn't want it to cloud her time with Antonius.

"No," he answered, lifting his head from her neck to stare down at her. His eyes, nothing more than dark pockets against his skin in the low moonlight, captured her in his intense gaze. His hands rustled against the grass, moving to her hair to cup her head and force her to stare back. "No, not for a roll in the grass. For any and every possible moment I can have with you."

Her fingers moved to his face, tracing the sharp line of his nose, the curve of his full lips, still swollen from their kisses.

"'Tis dangerous," she repeated in her heady whisper. "What do we do now? If we seek more than this one moment?"

His lips twitched against her fingertip.

"That I don't know. All I know is I want to see you again, as soon as I can. Mayhap, once the Roman army is dealt with, mayhap I can, we can . . . ."

Muireall pressed her finger hard against his lips to silence him. "'Tis too many mayhaps. I am fine with ye as we are now. Only the goddess knows what the future will hold."

He dipped his head to capture her lips again. He tugged at her lower lip with his teeth before releasing it.

"I will pray to my gods that my future will hold you."

Muireall waited in the cool grass, watching the faint red outline of Antonius run south, back toward the wall. That cursed, Roman wall.

But, she realized as she stood and brushed any grass or debris reminders of her interlude with Antonius from her skirts, if not for that wall, she wouldn't have Antonius, he of the sharp nose and intense eyes.

Oh, but the Great Goddess had an odd sense of humor.

The moon was high in the night sky, and Muireall had to hope her village slept. If the guard lingered at the gate and stopped her to ask where she'd been this late at night, well, her private baths weren't a secret. She could claim a need to bathe.

Fortunately, Evan's form stood at the gate. His ankle was still wrapped tight, but with his older brother Edan on his other side, he was a formidable warrior. Yet his presence at the gate concerned her. He was still injured. Did that mean their chieftain, Ru, didn't take the Roman threat seriously? Or was he just confident that he'd overcome any possible Roman threat? Or worse, was he worried about an eminent attack and pulling all his warriors into work, even an injured one like Evan?

Antonius's words echoed in her head, and she chewed at her lip as she approached the village gate.

"Muireall? Is that ye?" Evan's clear voice carried through the night.

"Aye, 'tis me," she answered and raised her hand in greeting.

"Och, lass, please tell me ye were no' wandering or bathing by yourself this late?" His concern for her was evident by the pitch of his voice, and Muireall patted his arm to assuage his fears, as valid as they might be.

"Ye know me, Evan. I worked up a sweat today. And the loch is no' so far away. I was fine."

Evan's jaw clenched as his eyes bore into her. Out of concern or disbelief? Suddenly, Muireall felt as if evidence of her laying with the Roman was painted on her skin as thick as blue woad.

"Fine, ye say. Ye should be grateful ye came home unaccosted. What if the Romans came upon ye as they did with us in the woods? Where would ye be then?"

She placed a hand on her hip. "Really? That Roman was ready to wet himself. I highly doubt I should fear the likes of him."

Fear naught but my own misplaced emotions, she thought bitterly.

Evan shook his head but stepped to the side to let her through the gate. "Please, next time, go in the day, and bring someone with ye. Gwyneth would be a fine choice."

Of course she would. If Antonius had feared Gwyneth with a sword, he'd run for the wall if she turned her bow upon his person.

Muireall nodded, feigning compliance with his recommendation, and patted his arm again as she slipped past him into the village proper. A path of beaten down grass led past the sheep pens toward the collection of roundhouses scattered throughout the village in flickering torchlight. She veered left, past the chieftain's house toward home, when another shadow emerged in front of her.

"Where have ye been?" Gwyneth hissed.

Muireall hung her head. Another confrontation about her whereabouts. Was nothing to be a secret in this village?

"Your mother was looking for ye after supper, and I had to tell her ye were sewing with Maeve at our hearth. Ye are fortunate she believed me. I would have hated if she confronted my second-mother, Tege, and my father found out. He might reprimand ye, but oh, he'd flay my flesh for lying to him!"

Gwyneth's voice was an angry whisper, and her urgency prompted Muireall to take Gwyneth's hand in hers to soothe her.

"My apologies, my dear friend. I thank ye for your lie. It saved my mother much worry, I wager. And I won't do it again."

Gwyneth's eyes were thin slits and narrowed more, her green eyes obscured by her hooded lids and disbelief.

"Ye weren't swimming. Your hair —" She reached out and wrapped a dry curl around her finger. "Ye weren't bathing at all. Muireall! Ye were with him? That Roman?"

Her mouth hung open, and Muireall had to resist the urge to press it closed with her fingertips. At this moment, she decided to do something she'd never done before. She lied to Gwyneth.

"He left a sign that he might have a message for me. I did no' know what the message might be, so I went to meet him."

Gwyneth's hand clutched hers, crushing it. "Muireall! Ye met that Roman by yourself? What were ye thinking!"

"He wasn't there," Muireall lied. Better to keep her meeting with the Roman quiet until he actually brought her useful information. Otherwise, her chieftain might order her to stay in the village, and he'd keep her there under guard. And she'd already made up her mind to meet Antonius again, no matter what it took, enemy or not. "I don't know if I missed him or if I misread the signal, but I walked out there, waited, dipped my feet in the loch, and came home."

Muireall tried to keep her eyes leveled on her friend, but even as the lie poured from her lips with ease, she couldn't look at Gwyneth as she told it. Muireall hated keeping secrets from her dear friend, and her eyes shifted away. Yet Gwyneth must have believed some part of her tale, because her grip on Muireall's hand loosened.

"As long as ye promise to bring me or another warrior, even Evan with his sore ankle, as some measure of protection. Ye dinna know what that Roman might do if he encounters ye alone. I saw how he looked at ye, Muireall."

Muireall nodded, keeping her face lowered. *Oh, if ye only knew what he wanted with me. . .*

"Aye, I promise," Muireall lied again, her voice breaking. The words were bitter on her tongue.

Gwyneth patted at her hand before releasing it. "Well, then, get ye home. Your mother will be wondering how much sewing ye were doing. Tell her ye were working on a new plaid with Maeve and got talking about her upcoming nuptials."

Muireall nodded in agreement and waited as Gwyneth gave her a tight smile before heading back to the chieftain's large wheelhouse. Then she was alone again and made her way home.

Her mother barely looked at her, giving her a slight smile and wishing her good eve before Muireall made her way to her bed platform behind the curtain.

At least her mother didn't ask any more questions. Muireall was quite weary of lying.

Chapter Nine: Secrets

Muireall spent the next day in a daze. All she could think about was Antonius, the feel of his hardened body against hers, the touch of his lips like fire on her skin, and the sound of his words that warmed her as much as his cock had. Every time she thought about him, a hot shiver coursed through her, and it was almost like she was in his arms again, reaching her heights under his writhing ministrations.

"Muireall, are ye even listening to me?"

Muireall's head snapped up and her cheeks heated again, only this time from embarrassment at being caught daydreaming. *Daydreaming of a Roman soldier, no less . . .*

"Muireall?"

She'd wandered off again! Her eyes focused on Gwyneth on the opposite side of the frame, the fleshing knife upraised in her hand. Scraping hides was a trying, unenviable task, and Gwyneth had thanked Muireall for joining her to help. Now here she was, woolgathering instead of working.

Muireall tipped her head down to the lower edge of the hanging hide and flicked her knife at it, as though she were helping.

"My mind is elsewhere, Gwyn. My apologies."

Gwyn's hand went back to the hide, scraping remnants off the edge of the fur, her eyes focused on her task and her lips tight.

"On the concerns with the Romans? Aye, mine too is distracted. My father met with his advisers late last night after I returned to the house. Dunbraith was most vocal in his desire for the tribes to unite and invade the Romans before they can attack."

Muireall nodded as her hands worked the lower edge of the hide, this time actually working to clear loose hair from the underside.

"Typical. When does he not want to invade the Romans? What did your father say?"

Gwyneth paused at her scraping and stood tall, stretching her back. She flipped her sunset red hair over her neck and lifted it off her damp skin, hoping the air might cool it. The complete lack of any breeze, though, meant it was a wasted effort. Muireall didn't blame her for trying. Sweat dripped down her back, and the cloth of her *léine* under her breasts was sopping wet and sticking to her skin. At least the grass had remained cool under her bare feet.

"Father was not in agreement." Gwyneth dropped her tresses so they cascaded down her back. "He believes the treaty will hold. The Romans surely recalled what happened when all the Caledonii came down from the Highlands and joined with the smaller tribes. He still giggles like a lass when he recalls the looks on the soldiers' faces when they encountered an army of Highland Caledonii warriors, naked but for the red and blue war paint on their skin and the spears and shields in their hands." Gwyneth shook her head. "Nay, he wants to add guards to the village and hold the Romans to their treaty."

Muireall flicked off a clinging piece of haired hide. "What do ye think?"

Gwyneth resumed her own efforts. Most of the hide was clear, smoothed and ready for treatment with soaked animal brains, and she crouched to finish the lower edge with Muireall.

"I was young when the Caledonii battled the Romans and sent them scuttling south to build their wall. I can see where Dunbraith makes a point. Better to press the advantage before we are forced to play the defenders. But then, I don't know all that happened during that previous battle. And I don't know what reinforcements the Romans may have at their camp now."

With that, Gwyneth looked over at Muireall expectantly. Muireall narrowed her eyes. "What?"

Gwyneth's hand stopped and she rose, her knife hand at her side. "Has your Roman said anything to ye? Anything about his camp, what weapons they have there, or how many men? Their intentions?"

Muireall's hand froze mid-scrape. Her back stiffened under her friend's hard glare. "What are ye talking about? What do you mean, did he say anything to me? I've barely spoken to the man, I've told ye!"

Gwyneth threw her knife down into the grass where the blade stuck hard. "Dinna take me for a fool, Muireall. I'm your friend, your oldest friend. Ye think I did no' ken that more happened last night than ye told me? Ye lingered at your loch far too long for naught to have transgressed. I saw how the man looked at ye, and I assumed mayhap ye had words, or mayhap more, that ye weren't ready to share with me. Or feared to. I know I'm the chieftain's daughter and ye are worried I might say something that raises my father's concerns. But dinna think me a fool, Muireall. Ye were walking on clouds yester eve, and today ye canna keep your mind on your work. More has passed between ye and this Roman than ye've told me, I'd wager."

Muireall kept silent and had a powerful desire that the ground open up and swallow her. She was hot with shame at hiding her actions from her dearest friend, at lying outright to the chieftain's daughter, and at knowing that she'd shared intimacy with the enemy of her people. What could she say? Nothing. Nothing that would make sense to Gwyneth. Though she didn't sound angry, she did sound concerned. As she should be. Muireall was involved with their most ferocious enemy, after all.

Gwyneth's warm hand closed on her arm, a tender, understanding gesture, one that extended to her eyes when Muireall finally lifted her gaze.

"I understand that ye may have powerful feelings for this man. I would for any man who looked at me the way he looked at you. But he's dangerous, Muireall. He's our enemy. Dinna get too close to his man. Get what information about the Roman movements as ye can, but dinna let him get too close, aye?"

Muireall hated herself for it, but she did it again. She lied to her friend and nodded. Her lips formed words contrary to her heart.

"Aye, Gwyn. I won't let him get too close."
Too late.

Muireall used the chaos of the sheep returning to the pens to sneak past the warriors guarding the front gate and ran like Cairbre, the god of speed himself, was chasing her toward the loch.

She had no assurances Antonius would be there yet, or that he would arrive at any time that night. When she reached the edge of the trees, the sun had fully crested the horizon and was tucking itself in for the night, and the stained crimson fabric fluttered in the graying light.

Was that a sign that he did want to meet her again? Or had it been forgotten the night before, left behind as Antonius walked back to the Roman camp? Her eyes watched it twist and dance in the breeze that had thankfully kicked up at sunset. She couldn't recall.

Yet, it was there now, and she'd wait until he showed up. If he didn't, she come back the next night and the next.

She'd keep returning until he came back to the loch, as ludicrous as that wait might be.

Muireall pursed her lips as she settled on a warm stone by the loch. Her desires and resulting actions made no sense to her. None. She'd had men before, boys really, with whom she had lain. But not a one had brought her to such heights, that made her insides quiver at the memory of a night to loving or the prospect of it. And certainly not one she was supposed to despise. They'd been green, thrusting boys, rutting to find their own pleasure.

Antonius, he wanted her to find her pleasure, for them to find it together, even when rushed. Muireall shivered again at the thought of him. Who was she fooling? Her body reacted with surges of ecstasy whenever she thought about his intense gaze, his warm skin, the movements of his body.

It was wrong, so wrong. Traitorous to her own people.

But she wanted him regardless.

She shouldn't have these lusty thoughts, but here she was. She'd heard Gwyneth's older sister, Riana, say once that one couldn't control the desires of the heart. Muireall hadn't understood at the time — Riana had fallen in love with a Roman herself and married the man after he'd rescued her from possible enslavement and a sinking boat. Oh, how the village and the tribe as a whole been in an uproar over such a thing.

Like many others, the idea of loving a lowly Roman had sickened Muireall when she'd heard it the year before.

Now . . . well, now she understood Riana's words in a way most others didn't. It would be easy to love one of the Caledonii warriors in her village. To love a Roman . . .

Muireall stiffened at the unfurling ribbon that was her thoughts. *Love a Roman?* Did she love him?

Surely nay — such a thing was not possible. She knew nothing about him but his name and affiliation. She'd met him all of three times and lain with him but once. What was that to build anything, let alone love, upon?

She chewed her lip. It was enough for her and her heart. As much as she hated to admit it, for her, silly lass though she might be, it was enough. She loved her enemy. She loved his rich, earthen-brown hair, his intense eyes, the sharp line of his nose and jaw, his rigid muscles strengthened by military work, and the pure pleasure his manhood gave her. She loved how his lips and fingertips made her feel more alive than she ever had before. She loved his tender words, his vow to protect her and lay his life down for her.

If she loved all that, she could see how she loved the man himself.

And if he didn't love her? If he were using her as one might use a camp follower, for his needs and that alone? Or worse, as a way to bring an attack on her people?

Well, she'd deal with that possible humiliation when it came.

Chapter Ten: Taking the Time

When they had lain together the night before, it had been a furtive meeting of bodies, of sheer need and passion and desire. Nuance was not to be found, and they'd barely undressed, only enough to satisfy each other in the most base and bodily way possible.

That was not how he wanted this night to go. As he came up on the loch to find Muireall waiting for him, he vowed he make her want him, crave him in such a way that their night of passion would never be forgotten.

Antonius had spent the day dallying around the Prefect's tent, and his efforts had paid off, at least slightly. Titus and a few other soldiers had been called into the tent. Though Antonius had strained to listen, he'd only overheard wisps and clips of the command. However, he hadn't missed the word *skirmisher*. A smaller attack to prepare for a larger siege battle, then. The day and time of that attack hadn't been spoken loudly enough for Antonius to hear, but he had something to share with Muireall, enough so that her people might prepare for an unexpected invasion.

Though the information tore at his insides, he decided to wait and share what he learned of the Prefect's intentions afterward. Her mind, her body, her desire, didn't deserve to be robbed of any distraction. Especially ones related to war, or that reminded her that he was a Roman.

Before he stepped out of the trees, he took a moment to study the stunning woman, barely visible in the night and shadows, her dress billowing around her legs in the cooling night breeze. She was like a rare and beautiful datura flower in the dark, blooming just for him. If he'd been smitten with her the first moment he saw her, he was completely lost over her now. How had this one woman stirred his mind and passions so? It was the stuff of myth, not reality, and not for the likes of him.

But here he was, ready for her.

Then he stepped out of the darkest shadows to join her, and she smiled and raced for his arms. They spoke no words; they didn't need any. Their breathing, their kisses, their bodies spoke loudly enough for the both of them.

Antonius thrust his hands in her tempestuous hair, wrapping the wild locks around his fingers and holding her head under the onslaught of his kisses. Crazed, fevered, biting and licking, as if the taste of her was the most divine spiced wine, the strongest snuff, and the more he had of her, the more he needed to live.

Muireall threw her head back as his bruising kisses skimmed her jaw and moved to her neck. He growled low in his throat as he nipped and kissed, and her arms tightened around the dense, tones muscles of his upper arms, her fingernails digging in where his bare skin disappeared under his red shirtsleeves.

Then she pulled away, and with a sultry and inviting look, she grasped the folds of her gray-blue dress and pulled it over her head. Even in the dim moonlight, the stark contrast of her milky skin as smooth as the fabrics from the eastern Roman borders, her full creamy breasts, and the curves of her belly that led to the russet curls at the juncture of her thighs made him lose his breath. His chest clenched tight with a pounding need. He panted as he watched her enticing movements.

She stood before him in full glory. He reached for her, but she leaned away and raised her eyebrows at him.

He didn't pause, realizing she was waiting for him to undress. He flung his tunic over his head as he yanked his footwear off with nimble toes. As much as it felt awkward for him, he also stood naked before her, letting her look her fill. His raging erection strained like a pulsing sword, searching for her.

Then the moment broke, and they rushed each other again, skin against skin, and fell to their knees. His mouth found her nipple, as smooth as the rest of her, and suckled on her copious breasts — ample, full, and unyielding against his lips. Then he shifted, cupping the lush rounds of her back side and wrapped his lips around the other nipple, teasing it with small nibbles and licks, and her chest heaved under his mouth.

With one brawny arm, he laid her back on the dewy grass, and played his hand down her belly, followed by his kisses. Then his fingers rested at the curve of her woman's mound, and here he paused. He lifted his face to her glazed eyes and raised an eyebrow.

"Once I get started, my love, I won't able to stop," he warned her in a guttural voice.

She lifted her fingers to his chest, cupping the chiseled muscle under his heated skin.

"Then dinna stop," she told him.

From the growl that escaped Antonius's lips, it was as if Muireall's words had released a beast inside him, one that would never be caged again.

His lips continued their path to meet his fingers that had spread her damp folds. Her thighs fell open, offering him her most intimate view. She tensed, her insides quivering as she waited for his lips to join his fingers. Spread open as she was, he readily found the nub of her pleasure, and in a deliberately slow curl of his lips, he pulled her nub into his mouth and grazed it with her tongue. Her fingers grabbed at the ground, clawing at the grass for purchase as her mind fell from her body in a whirl.

Her body was his to command, and he commanded it well.

He clutched her clawing hand, holding them immobile against her hips. Then he sucked, and her body arched off the grass, a shocking sensation as if every part of her body was being touched at once, and she emitted a high-pitched screech as she sucked in air.

Antonius moved his head, resting his swarthy face against her thigh where he kissed that feather-soft skin. His kisses marked her, scarred her, yet soft and pliant. His kisses were the perfect softness of beauty while his fingers released her hands and started their own movements, demanding and forceful against the moist, sensitive part of her. Everything about Antonius was conflict — his kisses soft and his fingers hard, his exterior a warrior but his insides smitten, her enemy and her lover. And she craved every conflicting aspect of him.

His thumb moved to her secret bud, and he rolled it around under the calloused pad of his powerfully skilled digit. She sucked in her breath again, another high-pitched screech as her body prepared for its release. She was writhing and panting and almost there. Then he stopped, his hand cupping her warmth. As soon as her eyes caught his, he did it again.

"Please, Antonius," she begged as she writhed under his skillful fingers.

But just as her moment built inside her, a storm ready to explode and shake the world from the earth to the skies, he moved upright and his thumb paused, slowed. His fingers shifted to slip deep insider her, first one finger, then another, then a third. She clenched her thighs tightly against his hand, as if she might force him to complete his dizzying work with her body.

Antonius chuckled lightly and licked at her dusky pink nipple.
"Not yet, my northern beauty. Last time we were rushed. This time, I'll draw it out for you until the gods themselves demand that I finish my task."

"Please," she begged again, and this time, he bowed his head to her lips, capturing hers in another delicate kiss. Just as he did so, his thumb moved again, his fingers still in her wet sheath, and the torture of his intimate touch was exquisite.

His kisses remained locked on hers as his finger worked her sheath and her nub until she was panting and arching off the grass.

"Not yet," he groaned into her mouth as he slowed his thumb.

She squealed as she squirmed, slamming her hands against his back, clawing at him instead of the grass, as if she could work her hips enough to force him to finish.

His hand moved again, faster this time, his fingers in and out, brushing against an interior part of her that was almost more sensitive than her woman's bud, and his thumb resumed its passionate stroking. Her arm slipped around his neck, locking him close to her, and her panting became a steady keening.

"Antonius!" she screamed so loudly that the goddess surely must have heard her pleading.

If not the goddess, then Antonius heard her, because this time his thumb and fingers didn't pause but rode out her waves until her screaming reached a fevered pitch.

Just as she found her moment and her body felt like the storm's thundering and lighting lit every part of her skin and every hair on her body, Antonius moved. His thick cock, so achingly thick, replaced his fingers, and he thrust in hard as her sheath tightened around him. She moaned at the tantalizing invasion. He didn't move, letting the constricting waves of her womanhood caress his iron hard rod. His head dipped close to hers as he reveled in her moment of ecstasy.

Then he began to stroke his powerful hips, keeping the same pace as his fingers had, and the center of her womanhood quivered again at his raw fervency. Every plunge of his swollen manhood was one of desire and delight, and she clung to him, wanting the sensation to last as long as possible.

His thrusts grew harder as his hips slid back and forth in a frenzied dance. His own breathing became a fierce panting as the muscles of his arms, chest, and shoulders strained. Antonius began to shudder against her thighs, and he threw his head back with an explosive roar as he slammed into her weeping sheath one final time, pouring himself into her in shuddering waves of passion.

Never had her body responded in the way Antonius made her answer the call of his own desire. Her world had tilted, changed, and Antonius was the man who had changed it for her. Their bodies surrendered completely to one another, and they sealed the imposing significance of this illicit joining with another gentle, soothing kiss.

"I should return. I'll be missed soon."

His arm clenched against her back, pressing her close as if denying he had to let her go before relaxing. Antonius exhaled against her forehead.

"Yes. I wouldn't risk you by keeping you too long. I should return as well before I'm caught missing. But first, I must tell you, I overheard Titus in his meeting with the Prefect, one that with only a few soldiers were in attendance. I couldn't hear everything, but what I did hear was that they are planning an attack, one that would be made to look like retribution for a non-existent attack on one of their Centauriae. And knowing what I know, that supposed attack was where we met you in the glen."

Muireall half-sat up, using her elbow for support. "How long until they attack? I'll have to share this with my chieftain."

"Probably within a day or two, from what I gathered. But if you are well-prepared, I have no doubt your tribe will fend them off with ease. And I will keep my head low and my ears open so that I might learn as much as I can about the attack. When I hear anything, I will find you. No matter what it takes, even if I'm caught." Then he placed his finger under her chin and lifted her face to his, duskier even by the shadows of the night. "You must know this. In my world, the one that comes to my dreams at night and distracts me all of my days, you would always be by my side, not running back to your village without me. And one day, I will make that happen."

Muireall's face tightened at him as she lowered herself onto his smooth chest. "I know what it is ye want. I want the same. But 'tis no' to be. How can it when ye are a Roman soldier invading our land? Ye will be executed by your Romans if ye are found by them, and executed by my tribe if we are discovered. What world do ye speak of?"

"I'm working on it. If we have to build a new world, mayhap that is what we do."

She grew quiet and traced the lines of his chest with a gentle fingertip. Mayhap his world was changed as well. "My older sister, she fell in love with a Roman who was our prisoner for a time. He escaped around the same time she was kidnapped by the Romans, and they put her on a ship to take her away. The Roman managed to rescue her and brought her home. My father gave his blessing, begrudgingly though it was, for them to wed. But she knew they couldn't live in our village anymore, so she now lives with her Roman in a different Caledonii village not far from ours."

Antonius studied her moonlit face. "What are you saying?" he whispered, barely able to catch his breath. Was she saying she might be with him, run away with him if necessary? The gods knew he'd give up everything — his position as a legionnaire, his warm homeland, his name even — if she asked. If it meant they might have a future that, at present, seemed impossible to have.

"I'm saying that a world in which we can be together, where we don't have to meet in secret and hide our loving, isn't an impossible thing."

He sat up at her words, pressing her backwards, and she rested her palm flat on his chest at his sudden movement.

"Would you be willing to do that? Leave with me? Start somewhere new? Do you —?" The word stopped on his lips, and her own mouth curled up at his hesitation. A sudden, hot frenzy surged through him, and he grabbed her wrist. "Why do you smile? Do you take this so lightly?"

Muireall's smile faltered slightly before she curved her fingers to grip at his chest. She marveled at how bare it was, scraped free of any hair.

"Nay, quite the opposite. And I was smiling to hear ye say it."

"Say it?" He lifted an eyebrow at her. "Why wouldn't I say it? Tell you how I feel? We've risked so much to share our bodies, should sharing our emotions deserve any less?"

Her eyes became hooded, yet that slight curl to her lips remained. "I've known ye all of four days. Ye are my enemy, and I barely know ye. How can ye have any emotions about me?"

Antonius shook his head. "That I cannot tell you. All I know is that, from the moment I met you in the woods, I've been consumed by you. Every thought I have is of you, and the more I'm with you, the more I want to be with you. So much so that I would give up my place in the world to join yours, and I'd kill anyone who tried to keep me from you. I don't know if that's love, but I've never felt anything like this for anyone else, and I'm willing to risk it all to love you."

Her eyes glistened, and she dropped her head, pressing a kiss to his chest. "It's so dangerous to love ye, but I canna help myself." She kissed him again, sending a shiver over him. Every time she touched him, his body reacted so hard that he nearly lost himself. He'd just had her, used her hard, yet his cock flexed, wanting her again. "But if ye are willing to take the risk, then so am I. I, too, have no' felt the same for anyone else."

He pressed his lips to her cool forehead. "Then it seems we are to embark on this dangerous undertaking together."

A rustling in the thicket beyond them made them freeze in each other's embrace. Without another thought, Antonius jumped to his feet, cursing under his breath. His sword rested on his tunic and sandals, out of reach from where he presently stood in front of Muireall, guarding her from whatever approached from the darkened woods. His mind reeled. Was it a lowly animal? Or had he been followed? Had his soldiers or her warriors discovered them?

The warm press of Muireall's hand rested on his back as she stood behind him, peering around the solid wall of his body at the trees.

Two men and a woman burst through the brush and darkness, weapons drawn. The red river of hair and fierce eyes of the woman was unmistakable.

Gwyneth, he thought to himself, just as Muireall spoke aloud.

"Gwyneth!" Muireall squeaked from behind him.

The red warrior woman wore little more than a sleeveless tunic that belted at her waist and barely brushed her thighs. Her spear was nearly as long as the woman, who was flanked by two taller warriors, built like hardy beasts and just as hairy. One man was the one he'd met in the woods — the one with the injured ankle that didn't appear so injured anymore. The other could have been the man's brother. He had the same brown, full head of hair and same broad features.

"I knew it," Gwyneth spat out, leveling her spear at Antonius's naked form, cresting from his chest to his exposed groin, then back to his neck. He had nothing but his bare hands, but he'd remain where he was to protect Muireall at all costs. Her friend didn't look amenable to Muireall's present situation. "Something about how ye were behaving tonight didn't sit well with me. Ye've never seemed that odd before. I'm glad I followed ye before ye made an even bigger mistake than taking this Roman dog between your legs."

Her eyes narrowed at him all the more, and Antonius stood taller. She eyed him up and down as if he were nothing more than offal. Muireall shifted to move around Antonius. He stuck out an arm to stop her, keep her behind him, but she lay her hand on his arm and set it back to his side.

"Gwyneth, 'tis no' like that. He's no' like the other soldiers —"

"Ooch, I'm sure he declared his undying love for ye before ye spread your legs. Do ye know the danger ye're in? That ye put the whole village in?"

Antonius gritted his teeth as Muireall hesitated, surely wondering if she should yet believe his words after her friend belittled him so. After all, she wasn't exactly wrong about the danger.

"Nay, Gwyn. He's willing to leave the Romans. And he brought more news. The Romans are —"

Gwyneth's face hardened all the more and swept the sharp point of her spear at Muireall. "Hush! Surely ye are no' so foolish to believe this lying dog! Leave the Romans? Serve as a spy in our village, most likely." She tilted her head at the other two warriors, and they came for Antonius, swords drawn.

"Gwyneth, nay!" Muireall shouted, lunging for Antonius before one of the warrior brothers grabbed his arm.

Gwyneth slipped the spear between the two of them and used the weapon as a bar across Muireall's shoulders, holding back her shrieking and struggling friend.

"What are ye doing?" Muireall screeched at the warriors. "Gwyneth, please listen to me!"

"Nay. I've listened to ye enough. We're bringing both of ye back to my father."

Muireall's chest fell into her stomach at that threat. Antonius shifted his attention from Muireall to the man who held his arm. He snapped his arm back as he twisted it, forcing it from the man's grip as he pivoted on the ball of his foot and brought his fist to the man's face, catching his cheek in with a solid, crunching punch.

The man's head snapped back, but he didn't let the hit deter him as his hand reached to grab Antonius's arm again. He seemed to almost absorb the hit. Antonius moved to punch the warrior again, but his hand stopped mid-fly, the strong hand of the other warrior catching it before his fist could land.

Antonius fought against the two men, kicking and lunging with a fury, but the warriors held him fast. The sounds of Muireall's shrieking filled the woods, and when he twisted his head to look at her, assure her everything would be fine, the man he'd struck got his vengeance and landed his own punch on Antonius's jaw.

The last thing he remembered was Muireall's pale, distraught face before his world went black.

Chapter Eleven: Confrontations

Antonius wasn't unconscious for too long, because the warriors were still dragging his limp, naked body through the forest. His feet ached and were slippery wet — cut from stones and bleeding most likely. His jaw throbbed where the warrior's punch landed with a vengeance

A flickering light appeared in the distance, and a sturdy wooden gate came into his view shortly after. Two more warriors stood at the gate, swords in hand. They were at the ready, on alert, and stiffened and gripped their weapons harder when the group burst through the thicket of trees and approached the guarded village gate.

His stomach dropped hard, flip-flopping inside him. He was walking to his death, that he knew. The best outcome he could hope for was that he made sure Muireall's punishment was the least pugnacious it could be.

"This the Roman?" one of the men at the gate asked.

"Aye, run and notify Ru. We'll bring him to the center of the village."

The man's eyes flicked past Antonius's head. "And what about Muireall?"

The warrior holding him shrugged. "Ask Gwyneth. She's her problem."

The man stepped to the side, permitting them entry while the other guard ran off into the village proper. Antonius tried to look at everything at once, committing as much of the village to memory in case he did manage to get away and could escape. The gate, the animal pens, the torches, the roundhouses . . .

Muireall was still behind him, presumably with Gwyneth, because he could hear her calling out and struggling.

"Nay, Gwyneth, please let me explain!" Muireall was still begging, and Antonius wanted to tell her she could stop, that her pleas were falling on deaf ears, but what good would that do? And he'd probably get another fist to his face for his efforts. If nothing else, he must keep his wits about him.

He needed to speak to their leader, convince him, if possible, that he wasn't a spy or the like, that he truly wanted nothing more than to end this animosity between the Romans and the Caledonii so he might have a future with Muireall — or prevent her from being executed for treason if that failed.

He *had* to make sure that none of the blame fell on Muireall, and he couldn't do that if he was unconscious.

"Best ye keep quiet, Muireall. My father will want to speak with ye after he deals with this."

"Please, let me speak to him first —"

"So ye can repeat the lies this dog told ye? I dinna think —"

"They weren't lies." Antonius risked a punch to speak. He'd not have Muireall's integrity dragged through the dirt along with him.

A hand smacked the back of his head. "*Haut yer wheest!*" one of the men snapped at him.

"Gwyneth!" Muireall's pleading voice called out again. "Listen to what he has to say! He knows the inner workings of the Romans, and what their intentions are! Please!" Her voice was so strained, it cracked. Something in her voice must have reached Gwyneth, because she didn't snap back but remained silent as she led her oldest friend toward the center of the village.

Other warriors and villagers emerged from their roundhouses to watch the naked Roman parade to the middle of the village. Though he should have felt some shame at his nakedness, Antonius held his head as high as he could. After all, these were people who fought in nothing more than red and blue paint — nakedness seemed to be a normal facet of their livelihood, at least in battle.

Yet their stares made his insides quiver — they looked at him with such animosity, such vile hatred, not that he blamed them. He could only image how their chieftain would look at him, just before he demanded Antonius's head on a pike.

A grassier area spread between a larger roundhouse and several smaller ones opposite it, and the crowd had grown impossibly dense. A public execution it was to be, then. Antonius hoped he would welcome an honorable death with the same courage that he'd shown entering battle in full armor. He had tried to live his life as one of honor, and if the gods recognized it . . . if the gods could be so kind . . .

The crowd hushed, and an immense man, not only taller than any man he'd ever met, but thicker, a wall of a man covered in wild, shocking red hair streaked with silver that covered his head, chin, and chest. The man was a walking red fury, and Antonius had to force his knees to hold still.

Then, in a moment of courage he didn't know he had, Antonius raised his head high and waited for the questions that would send him to his death.

"Wait! Chieftain Ru, I beg of ye, wait!"

Muireall's voice rose above the din as she broke free from Gwyneth's distracted grasp and rushed Ru, dropping to her knees at his feet.

"Muireall! Come away now!" Gwyneth demanded, grabbing at her gown that slipped through her fingers. Gwyneth had thrown her gown at her when Antonius had fallen limp, and now her *léine* was ragged and torn.

Muireall ignored her friend, evaded her grasp, and bowed her head to Ru's ankles. Her own wild red curls, richer and more burnished red than that of her chieftain's, fell around both of them like a blanket.

"My chieftain, please, I beg of ye. Permit this man to speak. He comes not as our enemy but to help us in the face of a betrayal with our treaty. Please, Ru, please listen to him before ye make any decision regarding his fate."

Her words, which had sounded so strong and convincing in her head when she'd practiced them on their trek back, now sounded frail and as weak as she felt. He was the mighty Ru Blogh, kin to the Caledonii King Gartnaith Blogh himself. What were her words to a man such as he?

If Gwyneth spoke up in her defense, perchance he might listen to his own daughter. But he'd already lost one daughter to a Roman soldier. The chieftain didn't seem ready to risk anyone else in the village to a similar fate.

Ru didn't respond. He remained rooted where he was, as powerful as the mighty oak, and surveyed the crowd and the naked, earthen-haired Roman before him. Muireall peeked through her cape of hair at her chieftain to see what his response to her plea was.

His gaze fell on his own daughter, who'd rushed forward when Muireall broke free and now stood right behind Muireall and in front of her father.

"What is this, Gwyneth? What's amiss? Does this have anything to do with what ye told me about a rogue Roman a few nights ago?"

His deep voice boomed in the night, and the low chatter of the villagers fell silent as they listened to what their chieftain had to say on the matter. It wasn't every day that a Roman was dragged into their village, and Muireall prayed to the Great Goddess that Ru would believe her words and Antonius's intentions.

"Aye, Da. He's the one who informed us of the Romans' designs to defy the treaty, break it, and invade Caledonii lands."

He exhaled loud enough for Muireall to hear him, and his legs shifted under her hair. "Muireall, get up. Go stand next to Gwyn."

She did as he bid, gathering her skirts and skittering toward Gwyneth who glared at her.

"Now, Gwyneth, why is he here exactly, and in a state of undress?" He raised one russet eyebrow at his daughter, and her lips pursed into a moue of distaste before she answered.

"I'd have thought his words to have merit, Da, if not for the fact that I, *we*, found him naked with Muireall sprawled atop him. Their situation suggests any information from him was only prompted by his desires to lie with a Caledonii woman."

Muireall's cheeks burned hard at Gwyneth's accusations. To have her intimacies with Antonius shared with the entire village! And worse, to suggest he'd lain with her only as a means to manipulate her, feed her misinformation to lead the Caledonii down the wrong path in how they dealt with the Romans? Her cheeks burned with both shame and hatred at the suggestion.

Surely, he hadn't done that, right? Surely, he hadn't lied to her as a means to spy on the Caledonii? Her lowered gaze slipped to Antonius, who stood with his chin high at the hard face of the chieftain. From the tight pull of his lips and his clenched jaw, he was also angered at Gwyneth's accusations.

A rush of cool relief flooded Muireall from head to toe. From the tense pull of his shoulders and defiant expression, he was just as insulted by Gwyneth's words as she.

He hadn't lied or used her! His words had been true!

And if he managed to convince *her* of his integrity from his mere stance, then he could convince her chieftain of his honorable intentions.

"Do ye speak our language, Roman?" Ru bit out the last word, which didn't surprise anyone. His daughter marrying a Roman only raised his ire with them more. He might tolerate his daughter's husband as he'd saved Riana's life, but that tolerance didn't extend any further. All Romans, in his estimation, were lower than dogs.

Muireall held her breath as she waited for Antonius to respond. What if he denied speaking their language as a ploy? What if he decided not to answer the chieftain's question and accept his deathly fate? What if . . . ?

Then his dark, sultry eyes shifted to her, and he held her gaze for several heartbeats, his entire face softening as he studied her, as if he was trying to speak to her with his eyes. She did the only thing she could think of to bolster his response, to let him know that she supported him in his conference with the chieftain.

She mouthed, *I love ye.*

His face shifted into something almost like a smile, a sense of smugness at her silent words. Antonius turned back to the chieftain, so Muireall saw only his refined profile.

"Yes, Caledonii. I speak your language, if haltingly," he answered in a firm voice, one of confidence, and Muireall's heart soared. Ru was nothing if not respectful of a man with a strong sense of control, and in this moment, Antonius exuded that.

Ru rubbed at his beard with one hand as he eyed the Roman, taking the full measure of the man.

"Why are ye here, Roman? My daughter believes ye to be naught more than a spy for your people, counter to her friend here, whose opinion of ye is slanted at best." Here his gaze coursed over Muireall as he pursed his full lips, then he returned his hard stare to Antonius. "Yet she has perchance spent more time with ye and might give more insight into your motives. What say ye, Roman?"

Ru crossed his formidable arms over that wall-like chest and awaited Antonius's response. Antonius took a moment to frame his answer in the best way possible — anything less would mean his death.

"Our Prefect is a man obsessed with power. He's not pleased with the terms of the treaty and believes your people can be subdued if an invasion is done right. He believes the treaty is a sign of Roman weakness and seeks to destroy it, believing that doing so will make him appear commendable to our Legate, and ultimately our emperor. I'm here because I believe in honor, that a man's word is his bond. To break this precarious treaty, that is something I cannot abide."

He spoke his truth — regardless of his feelings toward the Caledonii woman he'd come to care for deeply, he would have been against breaking the treaty no matter what. And he had to make sure this chieftain knew that.

Ru waited, pulling on his beard. "So what do ye have to tell us? What news did ye have to share that ye thought it prudent to search out the fair Muireall?"

From the way Ru intoned "search out," it was as if he announced to all those gathered that he'd done more than search her out. He had, but he didn't want Muireall to suffer for his affections.

"With the Romans, it's more than planning. It's preparation. The Prefect is mobilizing the men for an invasion of the villages just north of our camp, this one in particular. He figures if he attacks by surprise and defeats you, it will ignite a fire under Emperor Severus and lead to a larger invasion of the Caledonii lands by all the legions on the wall."

The chieftain stilled. Unmoving in the flickering torchlight, he reminded Antonius of a demon from Hades. Ru inhaled, puffing out his bare chest. The chieftain's man, a portlier fellow with a bird-like face, leaned in and whispered in the chieftain's ear. He reminded Antonius of a vulture he'd seen when he was a child, a ferocious bird with a puffed chest that had ravaged a piece of carrion on the side of the road. This man had that same look, a dangerous look.

"We know that your Romans are planning an attack. 'Tis why we have guards set around the village. What Roman will strike against our warriors? Not a one."

Antonius shook his head. The man didn't understand this wasn't a sword fight, a minor skirmish. This chieftain didn't realize what mobilization meant.

"Ye believe me wrong?" Ru's voice held a sharp edge, one that sent a shiver down his spine, and probably down the backs of those watching this fiasco.

"No, not at all. Look at me. Your very daughter managed to take me captive. But when I say mobilize, it's not a few Romans from a Centauriae on patrol. They might start with that, but if they meet with any manner of success, they'll launch a full attack. I mean the catapults and flaming arrows and battering rams. Machines of war that will lie low your walls and roundhouses and raze your village to the ground. If they elect to use them."

Something in his words, his phrasing, must have caught the chieftain's attention, because he and his man grew silent and stared at him. Ru's eyes flicked to his daughter and to the woman who stood next to her, the woman who had turned Antonius's world so abruptly upside down. From the corner of his eyes, he watched as Muireall met Ru's stare head on, not shirking from the powerful consideration of her chieftain. A swell of pride bloomed in his chest. If nothing else, at least she still at her pride. He'd sooner walk belly first into Ru's sword than bring shame to her.

Muireall wasn't shamed by him as a man, or at the fact he was a Roman, or that she'd lain with him. And if she could keep her chin up under the hardened glare of her chieftain, then he couldn't do any less. His face ached, but he focused his gaze on the chieftain's face and kept his shoulders as stiff and straight as his captors permitted.

"Ye are a poor Roman soldier to share your military secrets with us."

Antonius shook his head again. "Nay. A true soldier fights for what he believes is right, and disavowing the treaty isn't right. And if it means sharing that information with your village —" He paused and shifted his face to rest his eyes on Muireall's beautifully worried face. Her eyes blazed with purpose and intensity. "Sharing that information with the woman I love to save her, then so be it."

There it was. He shared it with the world, with her people, with her. Muireall would know that he put all he was, all he had on the line to save her and her village from his own ruthless soldiers.

The surrounding crowd buzzed, and Muireall dropped her eyes briefly before catching his gaze again and giving him a slip of a smile. Oh, how he loved that smile.

Then Gwyneth elbowed her, and Muireall's loving gaze shifted to her.

"Then ye are a fool. To give up your people for a sordid affair?" Ru scoffed, gripping his sword that hung by his side.

Antonius had the sense Ru would enjoy slaying him where he stood. "I don't agree with your assessment. It's anything but a sordid affair."

"Aye, a fool," Ru restated. He lifted his sword from his sheath with a clanging ring. His man leaned into him, halting his hand, and with everyone's attention focused on them, Muireall broke away from Gwyneth and rushed Ru again.

"Please, my chieftain, stay your hand!"

"Muireall!" Gwyneth chastised her. "Hold your tongue! He's our enemy!"

Muireall spun around, her skirts swirling wide. "Nay, Gwyn! He's not! He's risked execution by his own soldiers to meet with me, to tell us of this betrayal of the treaty, and ye are all behaving as though he's committed some grave crime!"

"He has!" Gwyneth yelled back, pulling herself tall against Muireall. "He's a Roman! On our land! That in itself is a crime! He's our enemy!"

"He's just a man!" Muireall countered, also yelling to make herself heard over her friend. "A man who wants to do what's right!" She spun again, grabbing Ru's arm that held his sword. "Mayhap listen to him first, listen to his ideas on how to defeat these soldiers instead of accusing him of treachery!"

"Ye silly lass," Ru spat out. "Ye are as foolish as he. Do ye think your sex is so fine that it might sway a Roman soldier from his duties?"

Antonius struggled and fought against his bonds and those holding his arms, trying to get to Muireall before her own chieftain laid a hand on her. "Muireall, no!" Antonius yelled. "I knew what would happen if I did this!"

Amid the chaos, a slender, ashy-blonde woman came up on Ru's other side and rested a dainty, braceleted hand on his upper arm. Ru's gnawing jaw stiffened, and he peered down at the woman. Antonius didn't miss how the chieftain's face softened slightly. Who was this woman? A sister? Nay, not red enough. *A wife.*

A wife who knew how to calm the beast that was her husband. Like the chieftain's man, she leaned in close and whispered in his ear. His jaw clenched again, and his chest heaved as he took a deep breath and huffed it out.

"Tege," Antonius heard the chieftain say. His voice was almost pleading. "'Tis no' the same thing."

The woman's fair eyes flicked to Antonius, then to Muireall, then back to Ru. She peered around her husband's burly chest at the portly man. "Dunbraith, speak to him that my idea has sense."

Dunbraith raised his eyebrows at the fair woman, obviously perturbed at the sagacity of whatever she'd said. Then he gave one curt nod.

"What she says has merit, Ru. We've aligned with other tribes with whom we've made war for generations. My enemy's enemy is my ally, after all."

Antonius pulled his head back. The man didn't look happy with the words, rather resigned, but if the chieftain's right-hand man and his wife advocated on his behalf, perchance he stood half a chance.

Ru's gaze didn't land on Antonius but shifted to Muireall and his daughter. He rubbed at his full beard.

"What has possessed ye to fall in love with a Roman, of all things, Muireall?" Ru asked in a tender voice. Muireall looked to Gwyneth, who shrugged, before turning to rest her gaze on Antonius. She kept her eyes on him though she spoke to Ru.

"The goddess's ways are a mystery. Who am I to deny her what she has wrought in my heart?"

Ru's jaw ground hard as he studied Muireall. Gods curse these Romans who were not only invading his lands, but the hearts of his people as well.

And he didn't trust this Roman as far as he could throw him, but Muireall seemed to trust him, and she'd had more interactions with the Roman than he. And while he hadn't met an honorable Roman — he was yet debating the worthiness of his eldest daughter's Roman groom — that didn't mean others had not. He'd heard disgruntled whispers from other villages that they'd encountered Romans who had left their legions, harboring a deep hatred at being sent so far from their homelands to fight a failed war in the north against people who obviously were not going to be subdued. They didn't want to fight and die in these cold, distant lands. This far away, they felt beyond the long reach of the Roman Empire.

Even his cousin, King Gartnaith, had encouraged the border tribal villages to work with the Romans and prevent any further antagonism.

And if Ru killed this Roman and sent his headless and cock-less body back to his camp, well, that would be taken as antagonistic, wouldn't it?

He worked his jaw and scratched at his beard, a common habit he had when thinking. His villagers watched him with eager faces. A call for blood was a fine form of entertainment, one his tribe reveled in, but then he flicked his eyes to Muireall, who stood next to his daughter.

This Roman had been giving them information about his own soldiers. Ru knew the risk that level of treachery involved — his people would nail him to a cross post in a heartbeat if it was discovered. If anything, the man had more to lose by being here in his village, being caught with Muireall, than anyone else.

Ru gave him a bit of respect for that.

When hadn't a man's cock led him down a road that could lead to his destruction? And yet, that man still followed those desires.

The air grew heavy with expectancy. Even Dunbraith was panting wetly on him.

Finally, Ru crossed his arms over his chest and looked down his nose at the dark-haired man with the bloodied face.

"I can make ye a deal," he told the Roman.

The Roman of the North

Chapter Twelve: Commitments

Antonius's head snapped up at the least-expected words just uttered by this chieftain. This red mountain of a man who could readily crush him with one fist, remove his head with one swipe of his sword, was speaking of deals? He shared an incredulous look with Muireall, whose own eyes were impossibly wide. Surprise? Pleased? Even she appeared shocked at her chieftain's statement. Licking his parched lips, he raised his face to Ru.

"A deal?" he asked.

Ru nodded. "I dinna trust ye as far as I can toss ye, but Muireall does, and my own daughter has shared some of what ye have told her with me. Until this moment, ye've given me nay reason to disbelieve ye, your Roman attachments notwithstanding, ye understand."

Antonius nodded. He well knew that his death would be assured if for nothing else than being Roman.

"In an effort to maintain an amicable relationship with the Romans, if no' your Prefect, I'm willing to give ye a chance. Ye've shared what ye know about the Roman plans. Do ye have an idea of how we might counter them? If ye help us come up with a plan of attack, I'll be encouraged to trust ye a bit more."

A rush of excitement threatened to choke him. He might leave this village alive?

"But I must ask even more of ye," Ru continued. "I also require that ye swear a blood oath to me, and to the Caledonii and our king. And that ye vow to leave your Roman life behind and live the rest of your life here. I canna have ye going back to your army and telling them of what we have in our village or where our villages lie, now can I?"

The tightening in his throat increased and dropped low to his belly.

What was this man asking? That he give up everything he had in the world to say here, in this chilly northern land? To not return to Rome, to his family, or to Mera? But then, they'd kill him if he said no. And what prospects did he have in Rome? None that he knew. Would the army ever return to Rome, anyway? He didn't know that either. And Mera? He hadn't thought on her since he'd met Muireall . . .

Muireall.

It was as they had desired — a world in which they might live together. Handed to him on a platter.

Antonius twisted his shoulders to look at Muireall, really look at her in more than just a furtive glance. She stood with her head bowed, her wild swath of deep red curls cascading over her shoulders, obscuring her face. She wasn't going to look at him while he made this decision. She wasn't a woman to beg or plead for herself. Nay, she'd plead for him, but her pride did have a limit.

His didn't. Not when it came to Muireall. Antonius faced Ru again.

"Do I have to dye my hair red?" he asked.

Ru's face hardened for a mere second before the white shine of his teeth emerged behind his beard. A huge, rolling chuckle, one as large as the man himself, burst from the chieftain, an explosive laugh made louder when his villagers joined him in his laughter. The blonde woman at his side giggled and hid her face in her chieftain's arm. Only the chieftain's second, the beak-nosed man, didn't join in. He was a man who was serious about everything, it seemed to Antonius.

"Nay, but ye will have to wear the woad and red berry, and mayhap some trews under your tunic in the winters, lest ye want to freeze off those tiny ballocks. Ye aren't ready to fight in nothing but your skin as far as I can see, yet. Your thin Roman body will take a while to grow accustomed to our northern weather." Then Ru's smile widened as he flicked his eyes from Antonius to Muireall and back. "Though, ye might have another way of keeping warm when the winter comes."

"My father is far too forgiving of these Romans," Gwyneth whispered in Muireall's ear.

Muireall raised her head, wondering if she really heard what Ru had said. It was well known that King Gartnaith wanted to find a balance of peace with these invaders, but to have her own chieftain of a like mind and to give Antonius a chance instead of slaying him where he stood? And Antonius agreed to abandon his Roman loyalties and join the Caledonii?

She flicked her gaze to Gwyneth, whose attention was focused on a dirt pile on the ground that she nudged with her shoe. Her friend didn't raise her eyes to Muireall, and from the look on her face, Muireall wondered if Gwyneth did indeed agree with her father.

The look on Antonius's face, however, a mix of surprise and joy, made Muireall's chest swell. Even here, naked as the day he was birthed and surrounded by his enemy on all sides, he held his head high and kept his nobility of spirit around him. Gwyneth couldn't deny how impressive that was.

Especially because Antonius was still buck naked. The Romans, Muireall knew, thought that the Caledonii way of fighting in little more than woad paint was a barbaric and perplexing practice, one that actually frightened some Roman soldiers, if the rumors were correct. Tunics, leg wrappings, armor and shields, these were the battle clothes of the Romans.

The Caledonii were so powerful and skilled, they needed no such coverings.

Muireall squinted an eye at Antonius. If that were the case, then he was fitting in quite nicely already.

She reached for Gwyneth's hand and squeezed it. "Thank ye."

Gwyneth's eyes, so much like her father's, widened as she half-turned to Muireall. "Thank me for what?"

"If ye hadn't stopped Antonius in the woods, threatened his life, and then let him leave with it, we would no' be here today."

Gwyneth rolled her eyes and shrugged a shoulder at Muireall. She might easily accept accolades about her skill with weapons or her abilities as a warrior, but when it came to more sentimental considerations, Gwyneth grappled with her emotions. Getting herself under control, she offered a slip of a smile to Muireall.

"Weel, so long as he knows, one misstep, and the next time he won't walk away alive."

Muireall squeezed her friend's hand again. Had any woman before claimed such a devoted friend as Gwyneth?

"Ye know how your soldiers think. What will they plan for an attack on us? How do these machines work?" Ru asked Antonius.

Antonius eyed the men around him. The chieftain might be willing to listen to what he had to say, but they weren't about to permit him a modicum of freedom. The two warriors, his right-hand man, and even Ru himself, kept a cautious gaze on him. But they had released his bonds, so at least he had that, and had sent most of the other villagers on their way while Ru and his men spoke to him farther up the yard near a large, flickering, stone-lined fire. Which he appreciated because they *still* hadn't permitted him to dress, and the night chill breezed over his skin, making it pimple.

Muireall and Ru's daughter Gwyneth also stood close by, observing Antonius's every move. Ru had given him a stick, and Antonius drew on the ground with it. Not quite the parchments that the Romans used, but it worked just as well.

"I didn't get the chance to overhear everything, sadly. Most likely, though, they'll send a scouting party first. They are called skirmishers, and their job is to make the initial fight, evaluate the area, and see where they might bring in their war machines." Antonius scanned the trees surrounding the village. "This village, it is quite secluded. And it's on a raised hill. Other than the main pathway, it will be difficult to bring in the war machines. And war machines would be hard to explain away if the Prefect was trying to claim we responded to an initial attack from you. So they will probably start with two or three *contubernuim,* about twenty to thirty men, and a shield wall instead. Just enough to engage you, wound or kill some of you, then justify a full assault."

"How do we fight a *shield wall*?" The word was garbled as Ru tried to repeat it.

Antonius shook his head. "You've seen it before, I'm sure. They use their shields as a wall, like this?" Antonius held up his arm as if he were holding his own shield. "It's the core of the Roman army, nearly impenetrable in battle, with hours of training and dedication to its structure by the soldiers. The wall is only as strong as a single link in the wall. Force the men to break up the wall, and they are as weak as any warrior." He eyed Ru up and down. "Mayhap weaker. Your spears and arrows can take them down if we can break open the shield wall."

Using the stick, Antonius drew in the dirt, explaining his idea. Ru's beard twitched as his lips pulled into a tight smile.

"I guess there is something to be said for Roman strategy."

"Naught more than what can be said about your Caledonii charge. We still haven't been able to repair the wall fully from your previous raids. The treaty is necessary to both sides, never believe otherwise."

Ru nodded sagely before slapping Antonius on the back hard enough to make Antonius fall forward. He caught himself before his face planted in the dirt.

"This is a good start, Roman —"

"Antonius," he interrupted.

Ru's smile widened. "Aye, best I start calling ye by your name. I won't be able to call ye Roman after this."

Antonius's dark eyebrows scrunched together. "After what?"

The guards on either side of him leapt at Antonius and forced the squalling man onto his backside. He looked frantically at Muireall, who just stood there, watching. She didn't even appear discomforted at his treatment.

"Muireall!" he shouted. She waved a hand in a smooth motion in the air, as if soothing him from afar. His insides melted as he struggled against the strong hands holding him down in the dirt.

Ru approached with a knife nearly as long as a sword in his hand.

"Wait! You said if I helped that you wouldn't kill me!"

Holding the knife over his chest, Ru stepped closer and stepped on his forearm. His bones ground together under the man's weight.

"Nay, I said ye'd have to give a blood oath, too. Now is the time, Antonius. Your answers here decide your fate." Ru crouched and lowered the tip of the blade so it brushed against Antonius's naked, panting chest. His insides were liquid, like swirling hot wine, and try as he might, he couldn't stop himself from shivering at this surprise confrontation with a wild barbarian and the prospect of death that hung like the sword of Damocles over his chest.

Ru let the knife hover for a moment. When he spoke again, his voice was impossibly deeper, almost an imperceptible grumbling, and Antonius couldn't understand the first few lines. A more ancient tongue? Then Ru's words became those Antonius understood, still deep and grumbling but at least comprehensible.

"Ye vow to abandon past affiliations and swear your life, your body, and your blood to the Caledonii, to swear your loyalty to your chieftain and tribe, and to welcome death with open arms in defense of her, until the gods and goddesses pluck ye from this world?"

"Yes." Antonius didn't hesitate. To hesitate would surely mean his death. "I vow."

His eyes followed the line of the knife where it dimpled the skin of his chest, and he sucked in, trying to pull his body from that deadly iron. He waited, expecting Ru to withdraw the blade, but he didn't — it nestled against his skin while he remained pinned on the ground.

Was there another part of the oath? he wondered wildly.

Ru's face leered over his, pressing the knife tip with more pressure against his chest — not enough to break the skin, but oh, so close. Antonius inhaled sharply and lifted his eyes to Ru's eyes that blazed hotter than a forest fire in high summer. Their intense glare weakened Antonius possibly more.

Had he done something wrong? What was the chieftain doing?

Then he noted that Ru's eyes flashed to the left, to where Muireall and Gwyneth stood.

"Nay." He heard the wisp of Muireall's voice and the sounds of her movements suddenly halted. Gwyneth must have intervened.

"And of Muireall?" Ru continued. "She is like a daughter to me, raised much of her life at mine own hearth. She is the single reason ye yet live. She has put her faith and trust in ye. Do ye swear the same to her? To put your trust and faith in her, to protect her against the dangers of this world, and commit to her, give your body to her and her alone?"

"Ru —" Muireall's voice pleaded, and she was shushed by Gwyneth.

Did she not want him this way? Was this a twisted Caledonii commitment ceremony? Or did she not want him forced to be with her, which is what this ploy by her chieftain appeared to be?

"I'll not have her believe I was forced to bind myself to her," Antonius found the courage to say to the man who held him at knife point. "Let me rise so I might speak to her myself."

Ru's beard twitched, either from displeasure or sardonic humor. He held the knife where it was, and with a sudden flush and a hiss from Antonius, he flicked the tip deep into his skin. Blood bubbled at the knife prick. Then Ru wiped his fingers on the tiny wound, and with a deft hand, wiped the blood across his own bare chest, then re-bloodied his fingers and wiped streaks of blood across Antonius's forehead and around his temples.

The blood oath, Antonius reminded himself. He hadn't expected it here, this night, and in the dirt, naked.

Ru sat back on his heels, moving surprisingly quickly and with agility for such a huge, older man. That one movement, more than any other, convinced Antonius that Ru was not a man to be trifled with.

"Now ye are marked as one of the Caledonii, and I'm marked with your blood to seal the vow. Dinna make me regret this, Roman."

The chieftain nodded at Antonius's captors, who released his arms. They tingled as feeling returned to his appendages. The fire of the outside hearth cast them all in shades of orange and crimson and flickering shadows, and his eyes went directly to Muireall, who resembled something of a red goddess, Persephone draped in crimson robes.

His mind had a sudden flash as he rose and approached her. Did the Caledonii have a goddess of beauty like Persephone? He'd have to inquire. Because surely that goddess's beauty was rivaled by that of the wide-eyed woman standing in front of him.

Gwyneth pursed her lips, but stepped back, leaving Muireall with him. How beloved this woman was in her tribe, to have the protection of her chieftain, the splendid friendship of the chieftain's daughter, and the collective backing of her village.

And here he was, a foreign interloper, invading their village and stealing her affections. What if someone in her village had wanted her? What if her attachment to him somehow lowered her status?

All these thoughts tumbled in his mind as he took her cool, shaking hands in his. She was just as nervous as he.

"Ye dinna have to. I never wanted ye to have to choose me. I —"

"Muireall," he interrupted in a rough voice made harsh by fear, exertion, and dryness. "I never asked you. I accepted what you had to give. But as I've told you, whilst I may have bedded you out of need, something about ye was more than that. I've felt a bond with you since I met you, something unexplainable. I swore to you that I was willing to risk my life by being with you, risk execution by sharing Roman movements with you because I'd not risk you, not for anything. And if you'll have me, I'd commit myself to these Caledonii, to this village, to you, for the rest of my days."

The blush of life and love tinged Muireall's cheeks even more in the firelight, and her chest heaved under the vee-neck of her stained tunic. Worry had crafted dark purple half-moons under her eyes, and her hair was a wild mass of chaos and curls, swirling around her head in a scarlet cloud.

But her eyes, her mossy, gold-green eyes made amber in the firelight, eyes overflowing with a pained mix of concern and hope, eyes that drew him in and didn't let go. Those same eyes that ensnared him that fateful day in the forest and clasped him tightly ever since, that's what forced his hand. Not a sense of obligation or a less-than-subtle threat by her chieftain. No, her eyes that spoke louder than any voice, gripped harder than any hand, and bound him tighter than any iron chain, those eyes that flashed at him now, they convinced him that he wanted this one woman more than he wanted anything in his life, wanted her more than even his own life. As Ru had intoned, he'd lay his paltry life down for her in a heartbeat if she asked.

"If you'll have me," he repeated, and with her hands, pulled her close so her panting chest pressed against his, and his small well of blood on his chest stained her tunic. Her body melted into his. It was like coming home.

She shook off one of his hands and reached her fingers to his forehead to brush at his line of hair grown shaggy in the Highlands over the past months.

"Aye, I'll have ye, all ye are and all ye offer. No more and no less. I'll have ye as ye are, Antonius, and I'll love ye all of my days."

His hand clenched against hers. "And I'll love ye all of my days," he answered in a rugged voice, torn by the depth of their emotion and the heat of the moment. Then he lowered his head to capture her lips and seal their future with one ardent, desperate kiss.

A throat clearing disturbed their private moment. Antonius lifted his lips from Muireall.

"As much as I hate to interrupt this tender scene," Ru commented with a note of derision to his voice, "we have plans to make." His eyes roved over the still naked body of Antonius. "And perchance find some trews that might fit ye. Edan, do ye have any that might fit our new villager?"

A flood of relief washed over Antonius, and Muireall's face brightened at Ru's statement. Edan cast a side-glance at Antonius, who was only a fingertip or two shorter than Edan, but just as powerfully built.

"Aye. I believe we have something that might work."

Ru nodded approvingly. "Fine. Ye gather some clothing for the bare-arsed man here, then we can rest for the night to prepare on the morn."

Antonius's head snapped up. "Um, I don't believe that to be a sound idea, Chieftain."

Ru leveled his hard eyes at Antonius. "Och, ye are in this tribe all of one minute, and ye believe to know what is best?"

"In this I do," Antonius told him, taking a short step closer to the chieftain. "Romans are not known for waiting, and they do like to attack in the early morn, before life fully encompasses the land, while their enemy yet sleeps."

The chieftain rubbed his palm over his beard. "Och, then. Get ye dressed. Ye'll have to delay bedding your woman. We have work to do."

Chapter Thirteen: A Plan in Place

  The villagers had everything in place and sat back in their positions, waiting to see if Antonius had been correct. If Antonius understood what he'd overheard back at the camp, and if he was as sure as he believed he could be about the Romans and their military strategy, then his expectation of how and when his Roman camp would convene on the village should be sound.

  Antonius rubbed at the sweat dripping down the back of his neck. *So many ifs.*

  He tried to tamp down his nerves that continued to buzz under his skin. He may have sworn fealty to the Caledonii and committed himself to Muireall, but in truth, Ru and the villagers had no real reason to trust him, no real reason to believe him, unless the morning played out as he suggested it would. While he didn't hope that the Romans would attack, it would certainly look a lot better for him if they did.

  Muireall was back deeper in the village with Gwyneth and some of the other female warriors who hid behind roundhouses and barns, lying in wait for any Romans who might breach the gate. The funny thing was, that was their intent. For the plan to work, it had to appear as though the Romans could breach the wall. Perchance if that worked, then they wouldn't use their war machines or get the chance to run back to their fellow soldiers and tell them to begin a full-scale attack. The Romans would all be dead.

The edges of the night sky transformed from the deepest indigo midnight to paler gray along the horizon. The sun had not begun to rise, nor had sunlight kissed the earth, but the bright, forthcoming of the sun chased away the shadows. In this dim gray light was when the Romans would most likely plan their attack. The Romans were wagering that this Caledonii village was sleeping after a long day of work or festivities.

Oh, how wrong they are, Antonius thought to himself.

Evan and Edan crouched to his right, a little bit closer to the gate itself. Their eyes narrowed and focused and their bodies tense as they awaited their moment to attack. The entirety of the village was quiet and still, with only a random low braying of the goats and the sheep.

Then Antonius heard it. And not just Antonius, but Evan and Eden shifted their bodies and gripped their weapons tighter. It was the rumbling sound of marching through the woods, and Antonius leaned in to listen more earnestly. He closed his eyes so the sound flowed to his ears more clearly. From the wrestling of feet, he estimated it was a *contubernuim* only, thirty men at most, not nearly a full century or cohort. If his count was right, then Antonius was correct that the Prefect was going to start with a lowly scouting party and save the war machines for a larger full-scale attack against many villages.

Why waste the time, effort, and ammunition of large war machines against one measly village that could be easily overcome? Antonio considered.

However, the Prefect underestimated the warriors within this one village, including the measure of the chieftain himself, who was like Zeus on earth. If the Prefect was leading this charge at all, he was going to be in for quite the surprise. And if their plan worked, and these Caledonii managed to subdue this troop of Romans, then the Prefect's plans to sever the treaty and invade the Caledonii would fall flat and lose support from any other ranking Roman officers. Antonius's lips pursed at the thought.

The rustling grew closer, maybe more *contubernuim?* Four or five groups instead of three? Forty or fifty soldiers? Antonius couldn't tell from the noise, masked as it was by the trees and brush. Across the way, the mighty chieftain Ru, clad in nothing but his shield, his spear, and body paint like every other warrior in the Caledonii village fighting alongside Antonius, tensed and glanced over at him. Antonius had elected to wear the trews he'd been loaned, but like the other Caledonii warriors, he painted his face, shoulders, arms, and chest in all manner of blue swirls and lines, blending in as a Caledonii himself.

Since he was, as of this moment, a Caledonii.

If the Romans could be defined by one word, in Antonius's estimation, that word would be predictable.

Antonius knew the Romans would use surreptitious movements and subterfuge to press their advantage, make it look like they were only defending themselves, and then use that guise to break the treaty and mount a full-scale invasion. And they would do it early in the morn to take full advantage.

From what Antonius had seen of the Caledonii, this Roman endeavor would be another unsuccessful invasion. A minor attack on a single village was exactly what his Prefect would do.

The rumbling sounds of marching grew closer and all the warriors hiding inside the village tensed. The misty air was thick and yet dark with night, even as morning chased the stars from the sky. Every Caledonii warrior was poised and ready to attack.

The distinct sound of shields and armor clanging in a steady march reached Antonius's ears. They were close, very close — it was time.

Ru looked across the gate at Antonius again, and this time, Antonius nodded. The chieftain lifted his hand with one finger pointed at the sky. Several Caledonii warriors went to work behind them, amid the increased braying of large Highland sheep. Antonius strained to listen, then the murmuring Roman voices carrying across the gate. He couldn't make out the words amid the sounds of the sheep, but he was certain one of them asked what *that* sound was.

The gate stood slightly ajar, and one of Ru's warriors, the exceptionally tall Niall, tugged it open a smidgen more to permit the sheep, now riled up by the excitable young *Imannae* who released them from their pens, an exit. For these younger Caledonii warriors, this plan was fine training on military strategy.

Antonius heard the rattling Romans come even closer, almost at the mouth of the gate, when the fluffy push of the sheep rushed past him and to the gate beyond, eager to search for an early morning meal of crisp grass.

What the sheep didn't expect was to run straight into a small contingent of Roman soldiers unprepared for an onslaught of sheep. Several men screeched out in surprise, which only confused the poor sheep more. The soldiers struggled to move around the sheep while keeping their shield wall in line, only to fail as more sheep butted against the muddled soldiers. The shield wall broke apart. Once the shouting and braying reached a fevered pitch, Antonius nodded at Ru, and he raised his hand again, this time in a fist.

Since they were busy trying to move past the herd of sheep that blocked them and distracted them from their target, the Romans were ill prepared for the flood of Caledonii warriors who moved easily around the sheep and were more than ready to take on the duplicitous Romans. Even bare naked, the Caledonii warriors fought with a shocking vengeance and agility, one that armor and heavy shields prevented.

A few of the soldiers managed to collect their wits and form a semblance of the shield wall, but it lacked a roof. Antonius's mouth dropped open as he watched bare-arsed Ru leap off the back of a sheep onto the slightly angled shield, stepping on it like it was a giant stair. With sword upraised and a wild battle cry that sent shivers down Antonius's back, the chieftain ran up the angled shield. Then he jumped over the crouched soldiers and landed with a sword blow to the back of the man who held the shield, widening the break in the meager shield wall.

Antonius joined the other warriors in moving toward that opening, slashing at any Roman he came across. Flicking his gaze back to the gate before pressing forward, he noticed that Gwyneth, Muireall, and several other Caledonii warrior women formed a line to guard the village from any rogue Romans who broke from their ranks for the exposed gate. They were a ferocious group — tight tunics that barely covered them, and nearly every inch of exposed skin painted in whirls and lines of blue, red, and green. No wonder the Romans hadn't made any inroads in the North — the barbarian women were as powerful and skilled as any Roman soldier. Woe be to any soldier who thought he'd break through *that* line of warriors.

He grinned to himself at the sight of his painted Muireall standing at the ready before turning his attention back to his own battle at hand. He made it to that rear of the contingent when a taller, blond man lowered his shield in a slight movement. The soldier's eyes glittered under the ridge of his helm and narrowed at him.

"Antonius?" the soldier asked, using his sword hand to remove his helmet. Titus stood before him, his face a strained mix of shock and disbelief. "What are you doing, fighting for the Caledonii, painted as they are?"

Antonius's blue-swirled arm lifted to hold his sword in front of his chest. "Titus. We've had our differences in this, and I know you would not agree. Breaking the treaty this way is a deceitful thing to do, and as a man of honor, I cannot abide by it. I believed you to be a man of honor, too. I chose to warn the Caledonii, and when they asked, join them in their fight."

Titus's eyes hardened into narrow slits. "You fool. You realize you'll be executed as a traitor the moment you return to the camp!"

"I don't plan on returning. I've sworn fealty to these people, and here is where I'll stay."

Titus scrunched his nose up at him. "Some vow, your fealty. You also gave a vow to the Romans."

"As the Romans did in the treaty to the northern people. I rather believe the Romans don't hold fealty in high esteem too much as it is. I harbored no doubt in aiding these people. In fact, my stance as an honorable man, one who stands by his vows, demanded it. If the Prefect held no value in the vow he'd made with the treaty, then my vow to him didn't mean anything, anyway."

"You were never worth your weight as a warrior, Antonius. It'll be my pleasure to remove you from this world." The taller man replaced his helm on his head.

Antonius bent his knees, ready for Titus's attack. "You can try."

He wanted to say he was prepared for Titus's sudden flurry of sword blows, but he wasn't. The soldier threw his shield down and grabbed his sword hilt with both hands so the full fury of his attack could land with the hardest hits.

Titus drove him back, one sweep of his deadly blade after another, until Antonius's leg struck the fluffy wool of a lost sheep frozen in fear amid the bloody chaos. Antonius bent backward over the sheep, trying to deflect Titus's barrage of blows. But his arms were tiring after all he'd been through over the past several hours. If that sheep didn't move, Titus would strike it dead when his blade found purchase in Antonius's chest . . .

Then a blur of shadowy blue coursed across his vision, and Titus's blows paused as he turned to face his aggressor. But he was too slow for the agile Caledonii warrior who'd leapt over the sheep's back and brought his sword down with mastery, right into the crook of Titus's neck. The Roman crumpled to the ground like a sack of grain.

Evan turned on his good ankle with ease and gave Antonius a cock-eyed grin. "Ye did us a service this day, preparing us for this attack. 'Twas the least I could do for ye." He grinned wider, then spun around on his uninjured ankle again, his sword at the ready.

Antonius joined him, but the battle was nearly complete. The Prefect had lacked any sense of courage in leadership — his body wasn't amongst those littering the pathway that led to the village gate. Most of the sheep had worked their way off the trail to the grass, and stood either shivering in blood-stained fleece, or chewed at the grass with their absent stares, as if the fighting was nothing more than another morning for them.

But not all Romans from the contingent were dead. Several had managed to creep past the Caledonii warriors and were making their way toward the gate. The women warriors inside the village shifted their stances, ready to take on the soldiers. Regardless, Evan and Antonius broke into a run, weaving past the lingering sheep and dead bodies, but it was no use. The soldiers would reach that deadly line well before any of the warriors in the trail could make it to the gate.

The women were more than prepared, and the bone-shaking sound of metal on metal echoed across the narrow glen. Gwyneth and her warriors held their own, with Muireall and Gwyneth together exchanging blows with one burly soldier.

His leather and metal armor, and his skill with shield and sword kept the women at arm's length. But it also kept their focus on him, and not on the other two soldiers sneaking up on their exposed backsides.

"Muireall!" Antonius cried out as he ran, his voice lost in the cacophony. She'd never hear him, and he'd not reach her in time. A stone closed in his throat as he watched the miserable scene unfold.

However, the chieftain to his right did hear him call out, and the mountain of a man swung around easily, his eyes searching the gate. In mirrored movements, almost as if they'd practiced, Antonius and Ru each threw their weapon with all the might their muscles could conjure.

Ru's spear struck its target first, slicing the Roman soldier at Gwyneth's back in the lower part of his neck, right through his red scarf. The spear pierced through his neck and extended in a bloody, dripping stump on the other side. The soldier froze with his sword arm uplifted and a look of surprise on his face. His sword fell from his grasp, and the dead soldier followed, landing atop his sword.

Just as Gwyneth struck her killing blow on the attacking soldier, the Roman behind Muireall lifted his own sword on the distracted woman. The soldier wasn't much taller than Muireall, and instead of striking his exposed neck, and Ru's spear at done, Antonius's sword flew blade over hilt and caught the man in the side of his exposed head. He must have lost his helmet at some point in the battle, and his skull cracked open with a sickening thunk.

Muireall spun around in time for the bloody man to collapse right on top of her, sword and all.

She knew she should have paid better attention to her surroundings, as she'd been trained to do. While most of the Romans were engaged on the path with the Caledonii warriors, and losing, another contingent had broken for the gate.

The fools, Muireall thought.

A Caledonii woman warrior was just as fearsome as a male warrior, and perhaps more deadly for being underrated. The villagers might know never to challenge Gwyneth to a fight, but the foolish Romans evidently didn't, and they succumbed to Gwyneth's spear and Muireall's sword just as quickly as their compatriots did to the blades of the Kilsyth men.

And she knew better — Goddess save her! It was something Gwyneth trained her on regularly. *Always sweep your surroundings in a larger battle! Guard your backside!* Gwyneth's words echoed in Muireall's ears, yet she hadn't obeyed until she saw the flash of the sword blade as it coursed over her head and landed with a solid thunk into the head of the man behind her.

The flush of relief she experienced was short-lived, however, and the force of the blade striking the man's head knocked him off balance, his sword yet tightly clenched in his hand. Instead of falling backward, which she'd expected, both the man and his dangerous blade collapsed atop her, and she screeched as a wash of blood poured onto her face, followed by the stomach-churning flap of half the skin from the man's skull slapping against her forehead.

Muireall recovered quickly and tugged at herself to move, but she couldn't, at least her head couldn't.

What's wrong? Why won't my head move? She felt no pain. Was she injured? What was going on?

"Muireall!" Gwyneth's panicked voice carried to her. She wanted to call out to answer, but with the dead weight of the soldier on her chest, she couldn't take in enough air to speak. His blood continued to pulse out of him, and she blinked red drops from her eyes and tried to move her head again.

Another voice came on the heels of Gwyneth's. "Muireall!" the deeper voice shouted.

Again, she tried to answer, but nothing came out. Then the dead soldier's body was yanked off her, and she saw the faces of Gwyneth and Antonius hovering over her.

"Antonius! Ye yet live!"

"That I do. Come on, let's get you up."

He reached his arms around her chest as Gwyneth tugged at her arms.

"Nay, halt! I can't move my head!"

Antonius's powerful grip immediately loosened, and he eyed her head. Muireall had a flash of fear that perchance she was more injured than she realized, that her head had been somehow struck by a weapon now embedded in the earth, before a wide smile broke out on Antonius's face.

"No, not your head. Your hair."

He reached next to her and twitched sharply. The dead soldier's sword, which had missed her head thankfully, had plunked into the ground when he fell, trapping her hair under the blade.

Though it had trapped swaths of her hair, it had also cut off several lengths of her tresses, which she noticed lying on the ground when Antonius helped her rise.

"Your hair," he said again, his gaze on her shorn locks.

Muireall patted at her wild hair, which had been made more unruly from the fighting to the point that the curls nearly stood straight up on her head, and smirked at the chunk of lost red strands littering in the dirt.

"Ooch, there's so much still on my head, I doubt anyone will notice."

Gwyneth hugged her backside fiercely. "Muireall, I am so sorry! I forgot to keep an eye out for anyone sneaking up on us, and it almost got ye killed!" she half-sobbed, half-screamed into Muireall's hair.

Muireall patted her with authority. "'Tis naught. Only my hair, and I have more than enough. I can afford to lose a bit."

Then she was pulled away from Gwyneth and wrapped in Antonius's nearly suffocating embrace.

"I thought you were done for certain. We killed most in the pathway, and we were so focused on them, we didn't see the other Romans until it was almost too late. There were more soldiers than I'd expected."

Muireall patted his cheek, her hands leaving subtle imprints in the woad and berry paint. The dried blood stripes on his forehead and temples had mostly flicked off, but fresh blood, Roman blood, stained his bare arms and chest.

"But ye did, and it wasn't too late. For my locks maybe," she said, kicking at one set of strands with her bare toe, "but no' for me. Ye saved me, Antonius, and helped save our village."

Then she rose on her toes in a quick movement and captured his bruised, battle-worn lips with hers.

The Roman of the North

Chapter Fourteen: A New Home

They didn't bother with any prisoners — the Roman lives weren't worth it. Dunbraith spoke lowly to Ru and Evan's father, Calder, near the gate as several young men dragged the bodies off to be burned in a pyre. Their visages were shadowed with the hopes that the black billows of human ash and rumors of the Roman loss in their subterfuge would frighten any other Roman who might have an intention of invading the Caledonii.

"What does this bode for the treaty?" Dunbraith asked in a low voice. Better to keep any suggestion of potential conflict with the Roman invaders at bay.

"That I dinna know," Ru answered, rubbing at his beard. "I'll have to send a messenger north to Gartnaith with this news. Is Edan up for the run?" Ru flicked his intense, mossy gaze to Calder.

"Aye, chieftain. Edan is always at the ready. He eats enough for it."

Ru's chest twitched slightly at Calder's assessment of his son. The levity after so dire a morn was welcome.

"I'll have him memorize a message to send to the King. We may have to reassess our arrangement with the Romans, or worse, prepare for war. But we are fortunate. This skirmish gave us insight into the Roman intentions."

Ru's gaze moved past Dunbraith and Calder to the dark-haired man, whose muscles clenched tightly as he carried a dead body past the gate. His mind spun as Ru thought of both this man and the man his eldest daughter had wed, another Roman soldier. Perchance the women of his tribe were thinking smartly, because those men offered another advantage in favor of the Caledoniis, one that Ru valued highly. Knowledge.

'Twas Antonius's knowledge that saved his village. They hadn't lost a single man or woman while the warriors of Kilsyth village had decimated an entire contingent of soldiers. That was something of value, to be sure. And Horatio, his eldest daughter's husband, had knowledge of Roman slave-trading and Roman ships that had saved his daughter from certain death. Antonius and Horatio, men who'd left their loyalties to a broken Roman military system in favor of the loyalties of their hearts. Other than the absurdities of their names, there was something to be gained having these men as part of his tribe and living in his village.

"As did Muireall's Roman. Before I send Edan on his way, I will speak with Antonius, see what other insights he might give us that I can share with the king."

His eyes followed the man, surprised at the turn of events regarding his engagements with the Romans. Never did he believe he'd have one, let alone two Romans living amongst his people.

Wonders never ceased.

Muireall's mother had hung a thicker plaid across the beam in her family's roundhouse to give Muireall and Antonius a modicum of privacy. Gwyneth had brought over several furs and wool blankets — "Gifts from Maeve," she explained — to add to Muireall's bedding. Given all of Gwyneth's suggestive griping about Antonius's Roman *invasion* of Muireall, she'd been more than generous and encouraging toward Muireall.

"I have to give him some credit for saving your life," Gwyneth huffed in feigned indignation. Muireall smiled at her. It didn't matter. Gwyneth supported Antonius and his joining Muireall in the tribe.

That, to Muireall, was a genuine friend.

She had worried that the Caledonii might not accept Antonius, given his Roman heritage, yet they had accepted Riana's Roman, so why not Antonius, who had just risked his life to forgo fealty to a dishonest leader and instead obeyed his own sense of honor to help her tribe. The Romans might be their enemies, but Antonius had proven he was not *her* enemy. Muireall blushed heatedly, thinking of what he was.

That night, after she had washed the sticky stench of Roman blood from her skin and hung her laundered leather tunic on the drying rack outside, she helped her mother prepare a simple supper as she waited for Antonius. Ru had called him to the chieftain's wheelhouse to glean as much information about any possible Roman attacks before he sent a messenger to the king. When she heard a disruption outside, Muireall raced to the low doorway and ducked outside.

Ru and his men walked Antonius to where the grass met the dirt-packed entry to her roundhouse. He grasped Antonius's forearm in a gesture of trust and appreciation. Then the chieftain slapped the younger, dark-haired man on the back. Antonius gave Ru a curt bow of his head.

"I thank ye again for what ye have done here today," Ru's deep voice rumbled to Muireall's ears. "But I must warn ye, though ye've taken the blood oath and shown your fealty to the tribe, it may be a while before other men, my adviser here included," Ru tipped his head to the tight-faced Dunbraith, whose somber expression never changed, "accept ye fully. As long as ye dinna let that get to ye, your presence here will be accepted soon enough."

Antonius bowed lightly again. "I think I can handle that."

Ru's gaze flicked to Muireall, who couldn't wipe the smile off her face. Even after such a rough morning and so dire a Roman encounter, the fact that Antonius was here in her village kept that smile well entrenched.

"And it seems that your woman is more than ready to help ye acclimate."

A hot blush burned at Muireall's cheeks, and Antonius turned to her, his own smile as wide as hers.

"Your statement holds much truth, and it's fortunate, since I plan on staying," he answered. His eyes softened like the feathery black down of a raven. Then he reached for Muireall's hand and looked back at the chieftain from over his shoulder.

"Now, if you don't mind, I'll take my woman to bed."

If you love this book, be sure to leave a review! Reviews are life blood for authors, and I appreciate every review I receive!

Love what you read? Want more from Michelle? Click the image below to receive free ebooks, updates, book discounts, and more in your inbox --

Get your free ebooks by signing up here!

The Roman of the North

An Excerpt from The Maiden of the Stones

Caledonii Highlands, 207 ad.

Fionn's dirt caked skin crinkled and flaked as he ran though the grove, side-stepping bright green, moss-covered rocks so he wouldn't slip. The water in the burn to his left churned in the late summer day, a gentle music that normally calmed his ferocious thoughts when they struck his mind.

Today, the music was lost on him. Today, there was only running, the flapping of his draping robes and the crush of the mud and grass as he ran.

Bursting from the thicket, Fionn veered right, racing through the field to the ring of stones that stood taller than he, taller than the mighty chieftain Ru in Kilsyth. The grass around the stones was scorched from the Feast of Alban festivities a few nights earlier. But it was a large oblong rock, half buried in the middle of the standing stones, that Fionn focused on.

He fell to his knees at the rock, sinking into the damp earth. From under his stained robes, Fionn withdrew his leather pouch and grabbed a handful of woad. He spat into the woad in his palm, and using his forefinger, drew a series of lines and circles onto the rock. Then he drew similar patterns on his forehead, the movements memorized and his finger knew the lines to draw. He dragged the woad in lines from his forehead to his cheeks until it touched his beard.

Fionn wiped the rest on his forearms and lifted his hands to the sky, sitting back on his heels. The chant that fell from his lips was at once old and familiar, but in the back of his mind, he hoped the vision he'd had was false.

The Roman of the North

The gods would speak to him, he assured himself, if he waited long enough. They would reach down from the sky and touch his fingertips and reveal to him if the vision he'd had was a fevered dream or something more.

Fionn prayed it wasn't something more.

The skies remained clear and bright with no message from the gods. They were silent on this matter, and Fionn clutched his chest, the pain of silence crushing his bones.

Dread followed, a dark, heavy cloak of dread that Fionn carried all the way to the village of Banton Loch, a much slower trek. The longer he could delay delivering this news, the better. The most he could hope for was that the chieftain of the Banton Caledonii wouldn't believe him. So few of the tribes today did — they saw Fionn as nothing more than a figure head, not a *Druidai* in the old sense of the word.

That didn't make him any less a *Druidai*. And it didn't mean his visions lacked merit.

It meant he needed to be more forceful to make himself heard.

Look for the next book in the series later in 2021!

An Excerpt from To Dance in the Glen

Prologue: Northern Highlands 1296

    The thrum of the horses' hooves on the ground made the earth vibrate in announcement. The horsemen scattered all about the land, searching for a woman who had been missing for nearly a day. The woman's husband, Laird of the clan MacLeod, Colin MacLeod, was beyond distraught, bordering on insanity in his search for his wife, the Lady Caitir MacLeod of MacLeod. A tall, strong, beautiful woman with hair blacker than the night sky and the most piercing blue eyes a soul had ever seen, it was rumored that God himself crafted her body in addition to her soul, carving her out of the most coveted jewels found on earth -- sapphires, diamonds, onyx.

    More than her appearance, however, was her very nature. While she practiced Catholicism as all good Christians did, she was raised with a deep-rooted belief in the old religion and tied it to her Catholic beliefs. She used herbals and prayer to heal the sick, advice and prayer to help the souls of clansmen and women who came to the Laird for help. She was genuine and honest and would give her very last shift to a poorer soul if they needed it. It was oft said that she kept Colin grounded since Colin, though he was a full-grown man reaching nigh two score of years, could still be a rash and hot-headed man much of the time. However, just a movement or gesture from Caitir was usually enough to calm the storm that was her husband.

All these reasons and more made her the most loved person in clan MacLeod.

No one, however, loved her more than Colin. He was infatuated with her and did everything in his power to spend most of his waking moments in her presence. He scheduled hunts, farming, even his business for accounts on Market Day around Caitir and how often he could be with her. Friends and family made jokes about how Caitir led Colin around by his nose, or other body parts, but instead of growing angry, Colin laughed at the comments. He knew them to be true.

But today, it was not laughter that Colin felt, it was anger and concern, more concern than he had ever felt in his life. Even more than when his oldest had fallen off a tree and landed awkwardly. They feared that the future Laird would be crippled from a broken leg, but it turned out to be naught more than a twisted ankle, and the lad healed fine. This time, however, there was little hope that all would be fine.

The English had pushed farther and farther north at the insistence of King Edward Longshanks, and the sufferings of the Scottish people had increased thousand-fold. Men were slaughtered, women raped and maimed, children beaten, attacked, orphaned, or even killed. The recent events had sickened Colin, and while the English had not come as far north as Lochnora, they had come close. Now he feared that they had come too close after all.

Caitir had left that morning to find marigolds, which she claimed were good for headache and for keeping bugs off other plants. While Colin was not inclined to disagree with her either way, he worried for her health. She was over six months full with their fourth child, a late baby since Ewan, their oldest was nigh on 15 years. They both hoped for a daughter this time, and Caitir had told him she could feel it. She had not felt like the bairn was a girl with her other pregnancies, and they weren't, so Laird MacLeod and his wife were confident in this omen. She had been inside so much, sewing bunting for the bairn while a steady rain fell outside, but that morning the sky was clear, even if a misty fog hung low. Caitir convinced Colin that she was fine and would not go too far past the main road south of Lochnora, so he had naught to fear.

When she did not return for a midday meal, Sarah from the kitchen asked Keith (since called "old Keith" after the birth of his son, "young Keith," much to "old Keith's" chagrin) if he would bring a lunch to the Lady Caitir as Sarah had not seen her leave with any food, and what woman with a babe could go more than a few hours without any food? Old Keith rode off quickly and headed south, expecting to see Caitir walking back towards the keep. Soon though, he realized something was amiss when he reached the edge of the land of clan Lee and still had not seen Caitir, either on the muddy dirt road or anywhere in the grasses and trees close by. Without pause, Keith reined his horse around and rode at breakneck speed back to Lochnora, screaming for Colin at the top of his voice.

Colin was already overwrought at Caitir's disappearance. He knew deep in his heart that something was not right and assembled several men to ride into the woods south of Lochnora to search for his wife when Old Keith rode up in a panic. He told Colin that he had ridden all the way south to Lee land and saw no sign of Caitir, only of riders traveling the roads. Now Colin paled in fear, afraid that the English had come farther north than ever before. Afraid that his beloved wife had encountered them.

Colin split the search parties into two groups, one to head directly south with himself, and the other to ride with Old Keith toward the southeast in case Caitir walked far from the road. Colin thought this unlikely, but he was not a man to make assumptions. He wanted the whole of the area searched, and they would not ride home until she was found.

They split off south of the road that led north to Lochnora and south into the land of Edmund Lee and his clan. At one of the more recent Market days, the Lees had told Colin of sighting the English just south of their holdings, and that was too far north in Colin's consideration. He had heard of the atrocities of the English, and had a wife, sons, and a clan to care for. Any sighting of English skin was too much. All of this plagued Colin's mind when he heard shouting coming from the woods to the east.

Old Keith had his group spread out within hearing distance to better cover as much land as possible. When he heard one of the younger men in his group (was it Simon?) give a loud screech, Old Keith rode to the man's aid, only to discover the most gruesome sight he had ever laid eyes on. They had found Caitir MacLeod, wife of Colin MacLeod of MacLeod, mother of three sons, and beloved of the clan MacLeod, and Old Keith's first thought was how to hide her before Colin approached.

The English had found her. Caitir slumped at the base of a tree, her shiny black hair now matted with dirt and blood. Her golden dress had been ripped from her, and her chemise torn up the middle, exposing her pale flesh. Her breasts were stark in the clouded afternoon sun, and there was no doubt in Keith's mind that she had been raped. However, the obviously violent rape was not the reason for her death. That was a result of the giant gash in her abdomen where her babe had lain warm and protected until this day. There was so much blood, Old Keith had no doubt as to the fate of the unborn child, and he heard Simon gasp, "oh GOD!" then turn and sick up his morning meal into the bushes near his horse. Old Keith dismounted and walked over to the young man when his eye caught upon more blood under some brush only a few steps away. Peering closer, Old Keith then saw the second most gruesome sight of his life. Not only had the English killed the mother, the gash in her stomach was more than a death blow—it was to remove the unborn child from the belly of the mother. Old Keith felt his gorge rise as well, with the full horror of the scene falling on his head. *She had been alive when they cut the babe from her. Oh, God save us. God save her.* Old Keith quickly unwrapped his plaid from his shoulders and covered the bloody, dead babe in the bush. *I canna let Colin see this,* he thought to himself. *'Twill kill him as sure as I stand here.* He then turned to the others who were immobile with horror.

"Quickly!" Keith yelled to them. "Take your plaid and cover the body! Quickly, before Colin comes and sees!"

He'd barely completed his command when hoof beats resounded in the woods behind him. He turned and saw Colin approach with his small band. Colin pulled his horse up to a halt, then dismounted, silent the whole time. Keith moved toward him, but Colin put up a hand to stop. He moved toward his wife slowly, as if trying to understand why she lay there on the cold, hard ground. Then he knelt to her, and placing one arm under her head and the other on her slashed belly, Colin pulled her body to his chest and cried out-- a loud thundering cry of all the pain and anguish and horror that one man could contain. Then he lowered his head into that once shiny hair and cried like a child.

The men surrounding him did not know what to do. They waited patiently for the Laird of their clan to slow his tears. They watched as Colin removed his plaid from his shoulders and covered his wife as best he could with one hand, then placed that hand under her legs and lifted her to his horse. Silently he rode back towards Lochnora, slowly, with his proud head lowered in defeat.

Start the award-winning, sweeping Medieval Scottish Romance here!

<u>*To Dance in the Glen – Book 1*</u>

The Roman of the North

A Note on History

Not much is known about the ancient insular Celts of the Scottish Highlands. We have some of their writing on ancient stones, and some remnants and artifacts – including their conical wheelhouses. The ancient Romans wrote a bit about them, but other than that, not much is known.

The Roman of the North doesn't follow one of Ru Blogh's daughters. Instead, I had a flash of a story, one that didn't fit the sisters' narratives, and decided to expand on the world of Kilsyth that I'd already created. It's more of an enemies to lovers tale where soldier has to choose between his fealty and his heart. I adore stories like these.

For this story, I explored the idea of the continued conflict the Celts encountered with the Romans, despite a tentative treaty. With skirmishes and raids on both sides, the treaty wasn't worth much, and soon, Emperor Severus would just try a full-scale invasion again. The last three books in this series will lead up to that event.

I also hope I've done justice to the amazing beliefs and structure of the ancient Insular Celts. I have read about their myths, festivals, and history, but just like the ruins reflected in this story, we don't know as much as we would like about these ancient people that forged the Scottish Picts we are familiar with today – so some creative inventions were necessary to present the ideology, keep the feel of the time period, and fit the narrative of the story. I hope I've painted the Celtic history in the best light possible.

For the entire series, I've researched and done my best to reflect the culture and people of the time, of course taking creative licensing when necessary to fit the story.

The Roman of the North

A Thank You to My Readers –

Thank you to my loyal readers – for you I am eternally grateful.

A huge thank you to the myriad of websites and online sources that provided so much needed information, including many on ancient Scottish history, dress, and on the Celtic ruins.

As always, I need to thank my kids and family for always supporting me. Even though writing takes me away from them, they are my best cheerleaders. I couldn't do this without their support.

I also need to thank my Facebook groups and writing colleagues who provide guidance and advice when needed. We are a tight-knit group, and you all are so wonderful for helping me along this path.

Finally, and just as eternally, I need to thank Michael, the man in my life who has been so supportive of my career shift to focus more on writing, and who makes a great sounding board for ideas. Thank you, babe, for putting up with this and for being my own Happily Ever After.

The Roman of the North

About the Author

Michelle Deerwester-Dalrymple is a professor of writing and an author. She started reading when she was 3 years old, writing when she was 4, and published her first poem at age 16. She has written articles and essays on a variety of topics, including several texts on writing for middle and high school students. She has written fifteen books under a variety of pen names and is also slowly working on a novel inspired by actual events. She lives in California with her family of seven.

Find Michelle on your favorite social media sites and sign up for her newsletter here:
https://linktr.ee/mddalrympleauthor

The Roman of the North

Also by the Author:

Glen Highland Romance
The Courtship of the Glen –Prequel Short Novella
To Dance in the Glen – Book 1
The Lady of the Glen – Book 2
The Exile of the Glen – Book 3
The Jewel of the Glen – Book 4
The Seduction of the Glen – Book 5
The Warrior of the Glen – Book 6
An Echo in the Glen – Book 7
The Blackguard of the Glen – Book 8

The Celtic Highland Maidens
The Maiden of the Storm
The Maiden of the Grove
The Maiden of the Celts
The Roman of the North
The Maiden of the Stones – coming soon
The Maiden of the Loch – coming soon

The Fairy Tale *Before* Series
Before the Glass Slipper
Before the Magic Mirror
Before the Cursed Beast
Before the Red Cloak
Before the Magic Lamp

Look for the Glen Coe Highlanders Romance series, coming soon!

Historical Fevered Series – short and steamy romance

The Highlander's Scarred Heart
The Highlander's Legacy
The Highlander's Return
Her Knight's Second Chance
The Highlander's Vow
Her Outlaw Highlander
Her Knight's Christmas Gift

As M. D. Dalrymple: Men in Uniform Series

Night Shift – Book 1
Day Shift – Book 2
Overtime – Book 3
Holiday Pay – Book 4
School Resource Officer -- Book 5
Holdover – Book 6 coming soon

Campus Heat Series

Charming – Book 1
Tempting – Book 2
Infatuated – Book 3
Craving – Book 4
Alluring – Book 5 -- coming soon

Manufactured by Amazon.ca
Bolton, ON

36826283R00092